Passionate Love Legends of the Past

Stories of Undying Romances

DR. GEORGE VAREEKAL

INDIA • SINGAPORE • MALAYSIA

ISBN 979-8-88555-410-7

THIS BOOK IS DEDICATED
TO
HUNDREDS OF MY STUDENTS.

CONTENTS

ABOUT THE BOOK

Passionate Love Legends of the Past: Stories of undying romances is a collection of a few fascinating love stories which have even changed the course of history. They include some of the most popular and frequently heard stories of love and romance. These legends are widely adapted in various literary genres because of their powerful emotional appeal. The collection is not exhaustive but is exclusive because of the edifying features and historical importance of the stories. The legendary tales are re-told here as they are read and heard in popular versions in order to refresh the memory.

Author

Dr. George Vareekal

ABOUT THE AUTHOR

Dr. George Vareekal, M.A., Ph.D. [English]., M.A. [Political Science]., LL.B. [Gold Medallist]., D.Phil.,Dip.T., D.E.L.T. retired as the Head of the Department of English, Seva Sadan college, Burhanpur, M.P. India. He was a member of the Board of Studies Devi Ahilya University Indore M.P. and observer for Rajiv Gandhi Technical University examinations. He has published six books so far and a few articles on various topics. He is profoundly interested in Literature, Law and Philosophy.

BOOKS AUTHORED BY DR. GEORGE VAREEKAL

1. **JEAN PAUL SARTRE: The Existentialist Themes in His Writings (2016).** This book is based on the doctoral research work of the author. It depicts the influence of existential philosophy on literature especially on Sartre's writings. It provides profound insight into the life of the great philosopher and literary luminary.

2. **MY MALICE-LESS MEMOIRS: Reminiscences of an Ex-postulant (2017).** An autobiographical book and describes the author's early life, schooling, and the life in two seminaries. It frankly narrates his mental, emotional and spiritual metamorphosis.

3. **THE SAGA OF MY SOJOURN: Ruminations on my Life and Struggle (2018)** contains the author's reflections on family life, socio-religious life and professional life. The book is written on the bewitching backdrop of Burhanpur and its marvellous people.

4. **THE CULTURE OF HAPPINESS: Thoughts on Happy Life (2019)** the expression of the author's

perceptions on happiness. The book contains many valuable suggestions and tips on happiness.

5. **LOVE YOUR CHILDREN: The Essence of Good Parenting (2019)** co-authored with Prof. Dr. Rajkumari George, is about the need for holistic care of children. The book reflects the authors' views on responsible parenting. The pivotal theme is "Love your children; they will perform miracle".

6. **ASPECTS OF ROMANTIC LOVE: Thought without Stigma. (2021) Romantic love is a fascinating passion and an ecstatic experience. This book encapsulates the author's personal perceptions on love, romance, marriage and related ideas**

XXXXXXXXXXX

EXPRESSION OF GRATITUDE

I express my profound gratitude to my family, friends and well wishers.

INTRODUCTION

Nothing in the world is more fascinating than passionate romantic love stories. If there were no such fabulous love stories life would have been very dull and monotonous affair. Love stories captivate us because of the bewitching emotional elements inherent in them. Love is the only emotion which has the power of enslaving the mind of another person. Love can conquer anything and everything in the world. When love is romantic it becomes a marvellous experience. The powerful flush of love touches the core of heart and lingers in the mind like a pleasing fragrance.

This book entitled **Passionate Love Legends of the Past [2021]** is a collection selective love stories which are appealing to anyone with deep interest history and literature. History is full of fascinating stories and legends inculcating zealous romantic love. They are as old as human race itself. The saga of humanity is the saga of epic love and romance. If at all we eliminate the elements of passion, romance and romantic adventures from history and literature the remaining stuff will be utterly boring to hear and tedious to read. If the passion, infatuation and infidelity of Helen and Paris are deleted from Homer's famous epics **Iliad** and **Odyssey** the residue will be the extremely tedious narrative, the scary skeleton without flesh and blood.

Love legends appeal to us because they are made up of the refined elements of human nature. Since human nature is basically same throughout the world the legends popular in one part of the world captivate the people belonging to other parts of the world. Romeo and Juliet, Antony and Cleopatra, and Abelard and Heloise, although appear like Western love legends, they attract anyone across the world. The love stories of the Mughal Prince Salim and his paramour Anarkali, and the tragic romance of Sohni and Mahiwal, although Oriental, are fascinating everyone. The painful Persian love legend of Layla and Majnun has profound universal appeal and has become synonymous with enamoured lovers everywhere. The stories of the notorious womanizer and philanderer Giacomo Casanova's sexual indulgences are read everywhere in the world. Every man possesses certain traits of character of Casanova as a passionate lover and habitual seducer of women.

Love legends become popular because they are sodden with sensual, sexual and sentimental elements. These elements are contained in every love legends from time immemorial. They are found in the mythological legends of Cupid and Psyche, Orpheus and Eurydice, Paris and Helen, and uncountable similar legends. All love legends touch our hearts with amorous feelings and fine sensibilities because of these fabulous traits. These features make love legends attractive, inspiring, universal and unique at the same time.

Love stories are beyond the barriers of regions, religions, cultures and languages. There are hundreds of languages and many regions, religions and cultures in the world. It makes no difference whether someone reads the love legends of Shah Jahan and Mumtaz Mahal, Abelard and Heloise, Bajirao and Mastani, or Romeo and Juliet in Hindi or in any regional language in India, in Chinese in China, in Sri Lanka in Sinhalese, in Italy in Italian, in France in French, in Greece in Greek. The legend will have the same impact and influence on the minds of the readers and will convey the same message. The difference will be only in the intensity of the emotions due to variations in narrations and aesthetic embellishments. The feeling created by all such love stories will be more or less same everywhere.

The tragic and sentimental strains of love stories make them bewildering and bewitching. The tragedy of Anarkali, who was entombed in a wall for loving Prince Salim, or Anne Boleyn and Catherine Howard, the hapless wives of King Henry VIII who were beheaded, and many others like them leave the readers or listeners distressed and devastated. The tragic elements in love legends like these fill our minds and imagination with agony and acute afflictions. The tragic love legends result in the catharsis of our emotions as Aristotle said in the context of tragic plays.

The love legends re-told here are not exhaustive. They are selected because of their popularity and appeal from my perspective. These passionate stories are familiar to any student of history, literature and folk tales. Many love stories and legends appear in text books and students are enamoured by the fabulous tales. The stories selected are only a small portion of the huge stock of romantic love legends to which I am acquainted with in English as a lover of literature. Interestingly even small geographical regions with small population cherish their own tales and fables including love stories which are transmitted fabulously from generation to generation in the form of oral or written communication. Such marvellous communications are the pride of the people and their legendary legacy.

Although we read a love story for pleasure and excitement each one invariably gives an implied message. The story may give the message that in romantic love diligence and discretion are as important as passions and emotions. Sometimes it is important to apply the reason of the heart before indulging in the passion of the heart. If the lovers do not listen to the voice of reason of the heart they will fall inevitable into tragedy. Abelard must have thought of the consequence of loving a student because he was a teacher. Bajirao failed to understand the voice of reason of his heart before surrendering before a courtesan. The same mistake was committed by Mughal Prince Salim whose indiscretion caused the disaster of his beloved. They simply fell in love at first sight and by the time they had awakened they were in dire dilemma. It was impossible for them to overpower the terrible tides of romantic love.

The transition from a normal love affair to an enrapturing legendary love is filled with romance, scandals, adventures and tragic incidents. This makes love legends universally attractive and interesting. Hundreds of novels, poems, stories and plays have been written on the theme and plot of these legends. They are adapted in television serials, film scripts and flourishing social media platforms which are the most popular modern means of entertainment. The characters and protagonists in these legends represent the common characteristics of human race. Thus the mythological Cupid and his ilk have come to mean erotic love; Helen of Greece represents conjugal betrayal, Majnun means an enamoured lover and Anarkali is a paragon of sacrifice in love. The legendary Casanova is a representative of incorrigible philanderers and seducers of women. The powerful Tudor king Henry VIII is an archetype of a lascivious husband. The legendary characters are types like these ad infinitum. Each story is intimately felt as "My story" not simply as "His story." All legendary love stories will be cherished as the rich and marvellous heritage of humanity.

xxxxxxxxxxxx

ONE

CUPID AND PSYCHE

THE MYTH OF ENDURING LOVE

Legends, myths and fables are integral parts of human civilization. They abound in the stories and exploits of gods, goddesses, superhuman beings, demons and exotic creatures. They form the essential contents of mythology, folklores and fairy-tales. Gods and super humans appear as real human beings and engage in activities like ordinary mortals. We cannot imagine a Greek civilization without the rich and powerful mythologies and mythical creatures. Likewise Roman civilization will be dull and monotonous if it is bereft of the fascinating mythical couples: Jupiter and Juno, Neptune and Minerva, Mars and Venus, Apollo and Diana, Vulcan and Vesta, and Mercury and Ceres. We cannot conceive an India minus the spectacular pantheons of Indian civilization. The trinity Brahma, Vishnu and Shiva form the three- fold forces of creation, preservation and destruction. There are also depictions of multiplicity of semi-gods, super-humans, animals and birds in the fables and legends of every country. They are in fact the cultural heritage and legacy of a country.

Ancient literature is enriched by the fabulous stories of the gods and goddesses, men with godly powers, and gods with manly weaknesses. They form the essence of human thoughts and their names enliven the pages of great literary works. There can be no Greek culture devoid of Homer's Iliad and Odyssey. The Indian epics Ramayana and Mahabharata are replete with supernatural characters. The Old Testament of the Bible is filled with Prophets and men and women with divine powers. In short all ancient cultures and civilizations flourished on

Cupid and Psyche

numerous gods and deities among ordinary men and supermen. Even the modern art and literature abundantly employ mythical symbols and adopt mythical characters.

The gods despite their supernatural powers behaved like ordinary mortals. They are born and brought up like humans and engaged in all activities of human beings. They inculcated emotions such as love, hatred, jealousy, anger, and revenge, like ordinary mortals. They indulged in fierce wars and nurtured territorial ambitions. They loved, married and procreated children. Many gods were fastidious and led life of profligacy and luxury. All gods had their own specific domain and areas of operation. For example Zeus was the king of gods in Greek mythology and Jupiter was his Roman counterpart. Hera and Juno were the Greek and Roman gods of marriage respectively. Aphrodite was the Greek god of love and beauty and Venus was her Roman equivalent. Eros and Cupid stood for love and sexuality in Greek and Roman mythologies.

The love story of Cupid and Psyche is one of the most fascinating mythical sagas narrating amorous adventures of lovers. Cupid was the Roman god of erotic love, affection and attraction. Cupid is depicted with a bow and arrow, and was winged in order to signify the power of lovers to dream and fly through imagination. The power of Cupid's arrows to incite love has become proverbial. People fall in love because of the power of Cupid's arrows to pierce into the hearts of the lovers. Cupid stimulates lust, carnal desire, passion and sexual pleasure in human beings. According to myth Cupid was the son of Mercury, the winged messenger of gods and Venus the goddess of love known for her indescribable beauty. Cupid was sometimes portrayed wearing armour like that of Mars, the god of wars to suggest the ironic parallel between warfare and love affair.

Cupid's Greek counterpart Eros also carried a bow and a quiver filled with two types of arrows. There were golden arrows with sharp tips to arouse passion and desire, and blunt arrows of lead to ignite aversion and apathy. Eros as a pastime struck at the hearts of gods and mortals and played mischief with their passions and emotions. Likewise Cupid is said to have shot a sharp golden arrow at Apollo who fell madly in love with a nymph named Daphne. He then shot a blunt leaden arrow at Daphne to incite repulsion, thus making the amorous advances of Apollo a one sided affair.

Cupid had a beautiful female companion named Psyche which literally means 'soul' or 'spirit'. Psyche was depicted as the youngest of the three beautiful daughters of an anonymous king in Greek mythology. Psyche was known for her matchless beauty and captivating appearance. She outshined even the queen of beauty Venus and people from far and wide admired her bewitching charm. The common people were enamoured by her ecstatic splendour and started worshipping her as their deity. Hitherto Venus (Aphrodite) was the paragon of beauty and people worshipped her as their goddess. But gradually the common folk began to shift their loyalty and devotion from Venus to the mortal Psyche to the chagrin and displeasure of the ascendant goddess Venus. She was annoyed and was overpowered by jealousy towards the new emerging idol of worship, Psyche who was only a mortal being and was not endowed with any divine quality.

Gradually people began to forget about goddess Venus and her temples began to fall to ruins. Venus became angry at the sudden and unexpected rise of a mortal princess. She saw psyche as an imminent threat to her own divine identity. Venus took the support of her own ebullient son Cupid to denigrate Psyche. Venus instructed him to pierce the princess' heart with an arrow and make her fall in love with the most despicable and hideous creature or an abhorrent monster. Venus told Cupid, "My dear son, punish that contumacious beauty; give your mother a revenge as sweet as her injuries as great; infuse into the bosom of that haughty girl a passion for low, mean and unworthy being so that she may reap a mortification, as great as her present exultation and triumph". (Cupid and Psyche by Lucius Apuleius)

Cupid decided to obey his mother's command. He went to the palace of Psyche. Cupid shot an arrow at her. When she awoke from her sleep Cupid saw her bewitching beauty. Cupid was stunned by her splendid radiance and bewildering beauty. In his utter confusion and alarm he hurt himself with an arrow and fell in love with her thus upsetting all the machinations of his mother.

Meanwhile Psyche's parents were worried about psyche because people worshipped her but no one came forward to marry her. People admired her but declined marital alliance. Psyche's father went to Apollo with his supplication for help. Apollo advised him to abandon Psyche on the top of a hill where she would marry a fierce and monstrous dragon. Psyche was deserted by her parents and sisters. However, she obeyed the instruction of Apollo and boldly went up the hill where she fell asleep. When she awoke she found herself in a royal mansion where she got a luxurious treatment. At night she enjoyed the intangible support of her invisible husband. She never saw his visage but was happy at the royal mansion.

Psyche expressed her desire to see her sisters who were apparently worried about her ever since her disappearance from the hill top. The god of western winds, Zephyr who was the loyal attendant of Cupid brought her to the palace of Cupid, her invisible lover and consort. However, her invisible husband told her to avoid meeting her jealous sisters. But she insisted and he agreed to her request. When they saw Psyche's palatial mansion and lavish way of life they were very jealous. They were surprised to hear that Psyche had never seen her husband. The jealous sisters instigated her to look at him secretly. They succeeded in kindling in her the natural feminine curiosity. One night Psyche, in fear and trembling turned the lamp and saw her husband's face for the first time. She was bewildered by the bewitchingly handsome Cupid. She was extremely sorry for her lack of trust. Cupid awoke and deserted Psyche because love could never survive where there was no trust. Cupid returned to his mother who again decided to repeat the revenge.

Now repentant Psyche wandered on the earth in search of her husband. She prayed to Ceres, the goddess of corn and harvest. She advised Psyche to surrender before Venus and request her help. But Venus was still nurturing jealousy. She assigned her many impossible tasks to reunite with Cupid. She intended to ensure Psyche's doom in the process of fulfilling the impossible tasks. The first task was that she gave a huge heap of corns and grains to separate overnight. Surprisingly a large army of ants came to the help of Psyche and she completed the task before time. Venus on her return was alarmed at the miraculous performance but her fury did not mitigate. The second task was collecting the Golden Fleece from a flock of sheep grazing by a river. Venus thought that she would drown in the turgid and turbid river or would be killed by the violent rams. But the reeds of the river helped her to collect the legendary fleece.

The third task was to collect water from the mythical rivers Styx and Cocytus leading to the underworld. Psyche disheartened by the difficult and dangerous task decided to surrender and end herself by plunging down the cliff. However Zeus pitied her and sent his golden eagle Aetos Dios that helped her to complete the task.

That was not the end of Psyche's ordeal to achieve her ardent love for Cupid. Venus was not appeased. She gave her one more task controlling her anger and frustration at Psyche's continuous success. She asked Psyche to Visit Persephone in the underworld Hades, and fetch a little of her beauty. That was indeed the most dangerous task since nobody could return from Hades. Here also she was assisted by the three headed mythical dog Cerberus who guarded Hades and Charon the ferryman. She obtained a box full of beauty but was not supposed to open it. However curious Psyche opened the box and found Sleep in it, not Beauty. Now Psyche fell on the ground overpowered by deep slumber as if she were dead.

All throughout her trials and tribulations Cupid had been secretly helping her. Cupid rushed to her and immediately put Sleep back into the box and Psyche revived. Cupid flew to Zeus who publicly approved his alliance with Psyche. He gave Psyche ambrosia the gods drink of immortality. Finally the marriage was approved by all. Psyche was awarded with immortality for her unstinted devotion and commitment to Cupid. They were blessed with a daughter who they named Voluptas which means pleasure.

The myth of Cupid and Psyche has ever since been emulated as the symbol of love, egotism, and carnal pleasures. Many writers have used the legend as symbols and allegory in their literary works. Sculptors, painters and artists have immortalized the legend in their creations. Psychologists have interpreted the myth to signify the psychic development of women and also to show the various aspects of erotic love. It elucidated that to become perfect woman must undertake a journey from the sensual to the superior level of love. Transformation of Psyche from mortality to immortality is the outcome of sufferings and sacrifices. The story ultimately envisaged a perfect balance of thought and sexual emotions of men and women. At the same time their love symbolized the primordial urge of sexuality in every human being and in every living organism.

The Cupid-Psyche myth has many dimensions to inspire passionate lovers and married people. There are many apparent themes and messages in this ancient and primordial myth powerful enough to inspire humanity.

(1) Love is a spontaneous and impulsive emotion. It is not a deliberate, pre-planned and calculated expression of emotion. 'Fall in love' is an appropriate phrase to reveal the spirit of love. Cupid's mission was to execute his mother's revenge on Psyche. But instead he was enamoured by her enthralling beauty. Cupid was hurt by his own love arrow. It was accidental but was destined to be because such was the electrifying charm and attraction of the mortal Psyche.

(2) The myth has a marvellous theme that love and trust are complementary virtues. Where there is no love there can be no trust, and where trust lacks, love will perish. Psyche must have trusted her invisible consort. Instead she succumbed to the envious insinuations of her sisters who could not bear the luxurious royal life of their sister. They could not compromise with the reality that their sister, Psyche who was condemned to live with a monster, was leading a life of luxury and abundance. It was their intrigues and instigation that led to Cupid's desertion and Psyche's consequent devastation.

(3) The myth unfolds the magnificent message that curiosity is detrimental to harmonious life. "Curiosity killed the cat" is an old dictum applicable to Psyche. It was out of curiosity that Psyche ventured to look at her bed-fellow. Cupid was awakened by the oil which fell on him. Again it was her sheer curiosity which prompted Psyche to open the box given by Persephone the underworld goddess. The box contained Sleep and while opening psyche collapsed under the spell of Sleep. Similar tragedy occurred to Orpheus who retrieved his love Eurydice from Hades but lost her because of his curiosity.

(4) The message of the myth is that Love can conquer all **(Amor vincit omnia)** and can subdue anything. Jealousy of Venus is obfuscated by the zeal of real love. Psyche's love was enduring. She had to undergo many trials and tribulations to foster her love for Cupid. Even gods and goddesses salute true lovers and enrich them with their blessings. This is evident at the end of the saga of Cupid and a Psyche. Zeus gave Psyche the celestial ambrosia, the godly drink of immortality. Thus Zeus acknowledged their love and made it immortal. The myth represents all the dimensions of love such as infatuation, intimacy, sexuality, surprises, sufferings, mystery, divinity and everlasting virtues. Love is blind and also dumb and deaf. Cupid is often depicted as callous and careless but was beneficent because he imparted happiness to couples both mortal and immortal.

xxxxxxxxxxxxx

Two

HELEN AND PARIS

THE STORY OF LOVE AND WAR

"Was this the face that launched a thousand ships?
And burnt the topless towers of Ileum?
Sweet Helen! Make me immortal with a kiss!"

These are the oft quoted words of Dr. Faustus the protagonist of Christopher Marlowe's famous play **Dr. Faustus**. The protagonist of the play Dr. Faustus wanted to have Helen, the Greek paragon of beauty as his paramour. Faustus surrendered his soul in order to have all what he loves to have. He bequeathed his soul to the devil in order to enjoy everything in the world. He demanded one thing after another in lieu of his own soul. Finally when he had the apparition of Helen in front of him he was enamoured by the splendour and grandeur of Helen's beauty. Dr Faustus only wanted to have a vision of that immortal beauty before his death.

He wanted to quench his insatiable thirst and curiosity before he handed over his soul to Mephistopheles, the devil of the medieval legend.

He had enjoyed everything in the world in lieu of the soul. He had conquered the world of profit and delight, and of power, honour and omnipotence through necromantic power. Dr. Faustus' vision of Helen was the ultimate fulfillment of his fascination for the mythological figure. Helen was the most beautiful and transcendent beauty ever lived on the earth. She symbolized immortality and sensuality. Marlowe wrote,

> "O! Thou art fairer than the evening air,
>
> Clad in the beauty of a thousand stars."

Helen symbolized the incarnation of beauty. The beautiful Helen of Troy was a legendary figure and was the first to show that a woman if endowed with extraordinary beauty could upset the politics of the world and frustrate the equilibrium of international state order. She was able to create ripples in the mind of Paris, the Prince of Troy and then controlled the destiny of two states, Greece and Troy, for about twenty years. The story of Helen was depicted in Homer's epics **Iliad and Odyssey**, and Virgil's **Aeneid.** She was married to Menelaus at a very young age through a competition of suitors in which Menelaus emerged victorious.

Greek mythology is replete with extraordinary men and women with supernatural powers. They are depicted in the epics with inscrutable attributes. Helen was the daughter of Zeus, the supreme god of heaven and earth, the equivalent of Roman god Jupiter. Zeus seduced beautiful Leda the wife of Tyndareus transforming himself as a swan and four children were born out of two eggs of the swan. They were two semi-divine children, Helen and Polydeuces from one egg and two mortal children Clytemnestra and Castor from the other egg.

Helen and Paris

Helen was destined to be the most bewitching beauty of the world. She was so beautiful that even as a child she was kidnapped by Theseus and hid her in the city of Athens. Helen's brothers rescued her and brought her back. As an adult she courted Menelaus who was wealthy and valiant. But Helen's love for him was tenuous without depth. During those days three goddesses were competing for the title of the fairest and the most beautiful of all goddesses. The three beauty contestants were Aphrodite, the goddess of love and beauty; Athena the goddess of wisdom; and Hera, the goddess of marriage who was also the wife of Zeus. A judge was appointed for the final decision.

The judge was none other than the prince Paris of Troy, a mortal known for his impartiality and fair judgment.

The three contestants offered bribes for a favourable decision. Athena promised knowledge and wisdom; Hera assured dominion over mortal realms; whilst Aphrodite promised the worlds' most beautiful woman, Helen. Paris decided to favour Aphrodite thereby inviting the anger of Athena and Hera. Paris went to the court of Menelaus under the pretext of a diplomatic mission to claim the prize promised by Aphrodite. He was honoured as a state guest and defying all rules of hospitality and good will Paris seduced Helen and fled with her in his ship to Troy. Helen did not resist as he whispered sweet nothings in her lovely ears clandestinely. Aphrodite filled Helen with insatiable desire for Paris. She forgot about her own husband, family and children and agreed to elope with Paris.

It was rather a ruthless betrayal of the host Menelaus, who was away to attend the funeral of his maternal grandfather. He was absolutely unaware of the surreptitious designs of his royal guest Paris, who spent about nine days in the absence of Menelaus. Those days were very crucial to decide the fate of two countries. Paris took undue advantage of the absence of the king and employed all means fair and foul to court Helen's favour. She too was fascinated by the charming personality and warrior-like appearance of Paris. Thus ultimately Helen deserted her husband and eloped with Paris to Troy without even a little thought about her unsuspecting husband and innocent children.

When Menelaus returned from the funeral of his maternal grandfather he learnt about the gross betrayal of his state guest in his absence. The episode infuriated Menelaus because it was highly insulting to the royalty and outrage on the integrity of the state, and the self respect of Menelaus as a husband. Menelaus decided to retrieve his abducted wife from the control of Paris. Helen's jilted husband Menelaus could not bear the insult and ignominy of his wife's betrayal. As a ruler he was bound to avenge the act of treachery. Menelaus under the powerful leadership of his brother Agamemnon decided to lead an expedition to Troy to retrieve Helen. Agamemnon was joined by a host of Greek Heroes and warriors like Achilles, Odysseus, Nestor and Ajax, and accompanied by a fleet of more than thousand ships.

The battle lines were drawn up, all for a woman. There were skirmishes and battles and death of many warriors for many years. Finally the Trojans were attacked by the Greek soldiers led by Odysseus, who entered the city hidden in the mysterious wooden horse known as the 'Trojan Horse'. Helen's seducer husband Paris was killed in the battle. As per their tradition Helen married his brother Deiphobus who was also killed in the battle. At last the Greek army traced treacherous Helen and returned with Menelaus to Sparta. However after his death she was exiled to the island of Rhodes by his step-sons where a vengeful Trojan War widow got her hanged.

A replica of the Trojan Horse stands at Çanakkale, Turkey

Menelaus was very angry, and raging at Helen's infidelity he was about to kill her. But she fell weeping at his feet and begged for life. Menelaus took pity and decided to take her back as his wife. There was however, another narrative. Menelaus could not kill her because of her irresistible beauty. Again there is another version. Menelaus surrendered her to the soldiers to stone her to death. But they were also stunned by her bewitching beauty and stones allegedly fell unknowingly from their hands. However Menelaus ultimately accepted her forgetting and forgiving her adulterous betrayal.

The most immaculate word love took a belligerent dimension in the love episode of Paris and Helen. An entirely personal emotion took an international dimension at the cost of massive loss of men and materials. The selfish interests and sexual inclinations of two individuals dragged the people of many countries into unprecedented agonies. Even Priam and Hecuba, parents of Paris could not restrain their love-laden son from advancing towards dangerous precipice. However his prophetic sister Cassandra had given many admonitions which they did not heed. Love inevitably was entangled in superstitions and excessive self-esteem. Helen's celebrated beauty was the cause of all sufferings, agonies and disasters.

Love as we envisage in the case of Helen and Paris was a conglomeration of intrigues, jealousies, rivalries, egoism and above all the anger of mythical gods. Men are simply, toys in the hands of angry gods. As Shakespeare said,

"Like flies to the wanton boys,
Are we to the gods,
They kill us for their sport" [Shakespeare **'King Lea**r']

It was a saga of ingratitude and betrayal, and exploitation of polity and good will of the states. There is nothing laudable about the audacious dalliance of the lovers. The love of Helen for the Trojan Prince, Paris was absolutely unjustifiable since it was the termination of the trust of her legally wedded husband and the oath of conjugal life. It was treachery and disloyalty towards the people who trusted her.

No doubt Helen was blessed with marvellous beauty and charm. There was an epic dimension to her ecstatic beauty. The writers from Homer and Virgil to Shakespeare and Marlowe were enamoured by the captivating beauty of Helen. Although she was a mythological character portrayed by the epic writers, Helen's unsurpassed beauty had fascinated generations. Her beauty was the source of inspiration for hundreds of people and Dr. Faustus embraced Helen as his spiritual guide and guard. He expressed his inherent feeling of adoration for her and implored her-

"Sweet Helen, make me immortal with a kiss!
(Kisses her) Her lips suck forth my soul;
See where it flies! Come, Helen,
Come, give me my soul again. Here,
I will dwell, for heaven is in these lips.
And all is dross what is not Helena."

[Marlowe –Dr. Faustus.]

Helen was the mortal and fleshy version of love, love in the voluptuous form. The love of Helen and Paris was romantic and subject to compulsions of carnal inclinations. Love for them was impetuous infatuation. They forgot their commitments to the family and society and thought only about their own happiness. They were culpable of pushing their states, Greece and Troy, to a long and devastating battle. The Spartan beauty and the Trojan infatuation would have been more laudable had they displayed restraint and moderation in their relation.

The legend of Helen and Paris presents a very different perception of romantic love. Love is infatuation without substance. It is nothing except physical beauty, glamour and skin-deep attraction. The love of Helen and Paris is appealing to the eyes but not to the heart. The so-called love was the disaster factor in the destruction of Troy.

Helen was the first woman to realize the power of sex to exploit the salacious and lustful rulers by hitting at their tender hearts. She was the Eve of politics who brought forth ruin by consuming the forbidden fruit. The lovers did not gain anything but managed to create many losers.

THREE

THE QUEST FOR UNION

There are many love legends in history depicting the innate quest for union of the lovers. The quest is irresistible and is the basic "do or die" tendency of the lovers. Many lovers commit suicide if they fail to fulfil their aspirations to live together. Sometimes unrequited love also leads to the suicide of the lost lover. However there are cases in which lovers embrace death as a matter of fate. Four such stories are narrated in this chapter because the tragedy of the hapless lovers fills our minds with deep sorrow and compassion.

(I) HERO AND LEANDER

The Helen-Paris episode is in striking contrast to another fascinating love story of Hero and Leander. Their tragic love story was one of the most painful true love tales of ancient Greece. Hero was a tall and beautiful girl whom the heart of any man could desire to possess. Christopher Marlowe depicted her as the incomparably lovely virgin. She was the priestess of Aphrodite and lived alone in the tower shrine of the goddess at Sestos on Hellespont. She fell in love with the astonishingly handsome youth named Leander of Abydos on the other side of the strait. They had at first met on the day of festival of the deity and continued to meet regularly thereafter. Leander was handsome, strong, athletic and an untiring wrestler and an adept swimmer. Every night Leander swam across the turbulent strait to meet his beloved.

Hero waited for her love on the top of the tower holding a burning torch to guide him on the perilous sea. She prayed to the goddess to watch over her lover when he swam the strait to meet her. Aphrodite had been very kind to Leander in his daring and adventurous journey to meet his beloved.

But unfortunately, one night the tempest rose very turbulent and Leander with all his strength mettle could not win through the willows of the stormy sea. He sank into the deep sea completely exhausted. The next morning Hero saw his dead body at the foot of the tower. She had nothing left for which she must live and so in utter dejection and despair she flung herself from the tower into the violent sea and perished. Thus the lovers were united in death. Their quest for immortal union was completed in their tragic death.

Hero near the dead body of Leander at the foot of the tower.

Hero and Leander were ardent and passionate lovers who embraced death in order to realize love. Love was not romance but a saga of sacrifice to sustain it. The goddess of love Aphrodite herself was the witness to their love. She liberated them from the probable problems of the future. She granted them death as a wonderful reward for their natural love. They died at the height of passionate love. Through death they immortalized love and gave the world one of the best touching romance tales.

[II] ROMEO AND JULIET

The tragedy of Romeo and Juliet immortalized by William Shakespeare is perhaps the most passionate and popular love story of the past. It has become synonymous with tragic romantic love. The two protagonists symbolize passion pathos and tragic discomfiture. The story has been extremely popular among people across the world and has captivated the minds of the youngsters. The popularity of Romeo and Juliet is due to its deep rooted sense of agony and sorrow of the two 'star-crossed' lovers of rival families. Although the story is based on a fable of antiquity, Shakespeare has brilliantly changed it into a fascinating tragedy of romance. He embellished the ancient fable with touching dramatic techniques, addition of minor characters and the use of beautiful poetic diction.

Romeo and Juliet

The plot of the tragedy is based on an Italian tale translated in verse by Arthur Brooke in1562 A.D. as The Tragical History of Romeus and Juliet. The same tale was retold by William Painter in 1567 A.D. in prose entitled Palace of Pleasure. The play has been adapted in many languages profusely for stage, film, opera dances and television serials.

Shakespeare idolized the two young lovers in the play and created them as paragons of romantic love. They are archetypes of unaccomplished love and represent pathetic lovers of all times. Shakespeare transformed the story into a heart-wrenching saga of sorrows and misfortunes of two ill-fated lovers. Romeo and Juliet became a ubiquitous presence in the world. They are omnipresent and are role models of modern Romeos and Juliets

The fascinating story of Romeo and Juliet is based on an age old feud between two powerful noble families. The feuding families are the Capulets and the Montagues settled in the Italian city of Verona. Romeo belonged to the Montague family and Juliet hailed from the Capulet family. The two families often engaged in aggressive quarrels and bloodshed thereby disturbing the peace of the city. The prince of Verona, Escalus had to intervene many times to resolve their disputes, and once warned the warring factions to banish them. The two teenagers of these rival families love each other passionately.

The Capulet family decides to give Juliet in marriage to Paris, a relative of the Prince. The decision of the family was not acceptable to Juliet. Romeo and Juliet already in ardent love secretly marry with the support of Friar Laurence.

Earlier there was a fierce fight between Juliet's cousin Tybalt and Romeo's intimate friend Mercutio in which Mercutio was killed. In anger Romeo pursued Tybalt and killed him. The Prince banished Romeo from the city of Verona under penalty of death. Meanwhile Romeo and Juliet met in the cover of darkness and consummated their marriage. "If love be blind, it best agrees with night."

The Capulets plan to speed up Juliet's marriage with Count Paris. But Juliet flatly refused. She took the help of the Friar who gave her a sleeping drink which made her unconscious and relapsed into coma. When the wedding party of Paris arrived they found the bride dead. Friar Laurence sent a messenger to Romeo explaining the plans and asking him to rush to save the girl. The message did not reach Romeo in time because of the plague in the city. Romeo misunderstood that Juliet as dead and he returned to Verona with poison and seeing the motionless beloved he consumed poison and killed himself.

When Juliet awakened from her stupor she found Romeo lying dead and in utter desperation stabbed herself with a dagger and joined Romeo in death.

Juliet's balcony in Verona, Italy, which is today a tourist attraction.

Friar Laurence recounted the saga of the two star-crossed lovers to the feuding families. The two rivals discarded their enmity and reconciled putting an end to all hostilities. They erected a great monument in memory of the tragic lovers. The tragedy ends with an elegy of the Prince,

"For never was a story of more woe,

Than this of Juliet and her Romeo."

The tragedy of Romeo and Juliet is a tragedy of mistaken understanding. The conventional plot has the stamp of profound sorrow and despair in it. The tragedy has resemblance to the Babylonian love tragedy of Pyramus and Thisbe, two lovers in distress due to the rivalry of their parents.

Romeo and Juliet immortalized romantic love through their communion in death.

[III] SAPPHO AND PHAON

There was another story which resembled the story of Hero and Leander. It was the one sided love Story of Sappho and Phaon from the Hellenic stories of love and romance. Sappho was an archaic Greek poetess known for her melodious lyric poetry. She wrote love poetry famous for its intense passion and description of love. Plato hailed her as the tenth Muse. Her attitude towards love attracted the attention of the people. Sappho was known as the icon of erotic love.

Sappho Reciting Poetry

Phaon was a boatman in Lesbos Greece and was very old and ugly. One day he ferried Aphrodite and accepted no payment. The goddess of love was very impressed by the beautiful gesture of the ferry man who was indeed a stranger to her. She gave a box of ointment in return of Phaon's liberal act. When he applied the ointment on the body he became young and attractive. Sappho met him at Olympus where she went to recite her poetry. Phaon was also there to participate in the competition as a charioteer. Sappho was captivated by the beauty and glamour of the young man and soon fell in love with him. When Sappho returned to Lesbos after winning laurels at Olympia she took the handsome, pleasant young man with her. Phaon was almost overwhelmed by Sappho's home and her way of life, and also her place of importance in the island. Sappho, deeply in love with Phaon tried her best to make him comfortable and at ease in his new environment. She constantly expressed her love for Phaon and told him how much he meant to her happiness.

Phaon was however ill at ease in the luxurious household of his mistress. He disliked the fun, frolic and merry making of Sappho's house. He could not tolerate the noise of the drunken guests. Phaon could not love Sappho as expected of him. Soon the one sided love became dull and damp. Sappho was unable to bear the unrequited love and romance with Phaon. In utter distress she jumped from 'the lovers' leap', a huge rock which jutted out into the blue sea and drowned. Her passionate heart was stilled forever in the fathomless sea. Phaon was quite indifferent and dispassionate. He soon married a beautiful girl who though not a passionate poet, was an excellent cook! Poets and philosophers are excellent moody lovers.

But no one can predict the duration. It is ardent but uncertain; deep but distracting; great beginning but often tragic ending.

Picture depicting Sappho jumping from 'the lovers' leap', to take her life

We get here an example of unrequited love. Sappho was the victim of apathy and indifference of her lover. She could not bear being bluntly ignored by Phaon. The unrequited love caused profound feeling of alienation in Sappho. Her realization that she was not loved by the person whom she loved ardently led her to suicide. The unreciprocated love always leads either to revenge or self-termination.

[IV] SOHNI AND MAHIWAL

The tragic love story of Sohni and Mahiwal which was very popular in Punjab region during 18th century Mughal period resembles the tragedy of Hero and Leander. Sohni, the unfortunate girl in the story was born in the potter family of Tulla, a Kumhar by caste. The happy family of Tulla lived on the river Chenab and was engaged in the pottery business. Sohni was extremely beautiful and was adept in the art of drawing artistic designs on the pots to decorate them. She helped her father in running the pottery shop.

It was during those years that Shahzada Izzat Baig, a rich trader from Uzbekistan came to Punjab on a business tour with his caravan. He happened to visit the pottery shop and saw the stunningly beautiful Sohni at the shop. He was enamoured at the very first sight of the bewitching beauty of Sohni. Thereafter he visited the shop every day to buy pots and earthen pitchers. Gradually Sohni also lost her heart to the wonderful customer Izzat Baig.

Love smitten Izzat Baig did not return with the caravan and instead took up a job in the house of Tulla, disguised as an ordinary man, to graze buffaloes. Thereafter he came to be known as Mahiwal or buffalo herder. Sohni was aware of her disguised lover and continued their romantic love affair secretly. However, they could not hide their love from the family and community for a long time. Love, like laughter is difficult to resist. Soon rumours and gossips were at galore about their love and secret romance. The affair caused great flutter and turbulence among the potter community.

It was a great crime and sin to love someone outside the caste and community. The parents of Sohni decided to marry her to a man from the Kumhar caste before the scandal became an ignominy to the family. Therefore, they arranged her marriage to a man from the potter community without her consent. One day the marriage party came with the groom and hapless Sohni had to submit to the temper of her parents and relatives. She was sent off to another village with her husband.

The distraught lover Izzat Baig was in utter despair and he renounced the world and became a hermit. He made a hut on the bank of river Chenab opposite to Sohni's new home.

Sohni was absolutely devastated and was unhappy with her new life. She despised the man to whom she was forcibly married. She continued to love Mahiwal now living disguised as a hermit on the other bank of the river. They met clandestinely in the dark when the whole world remained in deep sleep.

Sohni would swim across the river with the help of a hard baked pitcher. Mahiwal would come with a roasted fish regularly for his beloved. It is said one day he could not get a catch of fish. So he cut a slice of flesh from his thigh and roasted to feed his love. Sohni realized the depth and intensity of his love and passion for her.

Meanwhile rumours of the clandestine romantic meetings started spreading in the form of gossips. Their secret rendezvous was discovered by Sohni's suspicious sister-in-law who used to follow her secretly. She informed her mother about the secret adulterous behaviour of Sohni.

Now the two women covertly decided to do away with the unfaithful woman forever to save the family from infamy. One day when her husband was away on a long business tour the ladies replaced the hard baked pitcher with an unbaked one. The following night when Sohni tried to swim across the river with the help of the replaced pitcher unaware of the deceitful act of her sister-in-law, it dissolved and Sohni drowned in the river.

Sohni crossing the river with an unbaked pitcher

Mahiwal who was watching the tragic struggle of his dying love in the turbulent river, suddenly jumped into the river to rescue her. His efforts to save his beloved however did not materialize and ironically he too drowned in the river clasping Sohni. Their dead bodies were found next morning by fishermen. The ardent lovers ultimately united in death. They became immortal symbols of immaculate love through divine intercession. The tombs of Sohni and Mahiwal are situated at Shahdapur in the Sindh province of Pakistan, and are visited by lovers from far and wide. The defiant lovers are idolized by romantic lovers.

Four

ABELARD AND HELOISE

THE GREAT MEDIEVAL LOVE STORY

Medieval period in history had witnessed many heart throbbing cases of love and romance. Love meant love fabled and modified in stories, fairy tales, religious beliefs and scholastic philosophy. Many kings, queens, warriors, writers, thinkers, philosophers and pastors made history by their romantic inclinations and amorous adventures. They recorded their life of passionate love and real life romance. Peter Abelard and his intelligent student Heloise had a torrid and zealous love affair. The legendary king Arthur and the stories of his wife Guinevere, whose heart however was with one of Arthur's knights, dominated the medieval literature. Attractive and handsome Edward IV who captivated the imagination of many young ladies surprisingly married Elizabeth Woodville, a widow and mother of two children.

At the age of 30 Eleanor of Aquitaine who was the bold and beautiful queen of France divorced her meek and mild minded husband king Louis VII and married the young and brash 18 year old Henry of Plantagenet royal dynasty, future king of England. They had eight children of whom two became kings later on. Henry VIII married captivating Anne Boleyn, leaving Catherine for want of a son to succeed him. But ultimately their love and marriage culminated with the beheading of Anne. Henry VIII is best known for his six marriages and his efforts to annul his first marriage to Catherine of Aragon. His disagreement with the Pope on this issue of annulment of marriage resulted in the separation of the Church of England from the authority of the Pope.

Heloise und Abälard. Nach dem Denkmal von Durand.

The stories of love, romance, repentance and repudiation fill the pages of medieval history and literature. There is intricacy, complexity, tragedy, comedy and melodrama in each love legend of the medieval period. The main feature of the medieval love stories, with exceptions of course, was that it was the exclusive privilege of the kings, nobles, courtiers, and aristocrats to indulge in love and romance. The ordinary citizens, mortals who were subjects, were too weak to express their love. They dared not into any scandalous love affair and even if they did that was only a clandestine affair. Love was anathema and a forbidden act for the common man. In short love was a royal prerogative to indulge in lascivious love and passion irrespective of religious strictures.

A very exceptional and revolutionary love affair flourished between **Peter Abelard** (1079–1142) and **Heloise** (1098–1164). Their love affair and lifelong devotion to and correspondence with each other even after each had adopted religious habits, made them fascinating figures in the history of romance. Abelard was a keen and brilliant scholar and a philosopher of great reputation. He was a smart and charismatic young man. His scholarship and erudition attracted students from far and wide. Abelard was so confident of his scholarship that he challenged even his masters like Roscellinus and William of Chapeaux who were well-known philosophers of the time in intellectual disputations.

Abelard's dream girl was the young and beautiful student in her teens pursuing philosophical studies. She was lovely and glamorous with a keen mind and unquenchable quest for knowledge. She was none other than Heloise whose parentage was doubtful and she was raised in a nunnery at Argenteuil with her mother Hersinde, an unwed mother or a concubine. Abelard and Heloise were extraordinary individuals and were deeply absorbed in philosophy and literature.

Abelard was in his thirties and wanted to experience the joy of romantic love. He found in Heloise all those qualities to be united in love. Heloise was living under the protection of her uncle Filbert, a canon at the cathedral. He wanted his niece to have the best education and training in philosophy. He chose Abelard for providing private instruction to Heloise. This inevitably opened the door of Fulbert's house to the smart and brilliant professor. It was like a tender lamb being entrusted to the care of a ravenous wolf!

Physical proximity brought forth deep mental and emotional nearness. Thus the philosopher teacher and his young and ebullient teen aged student were inseparably in love. This unusual love affair scandalized the academic community and was a great challenge to the orthodox Parisian society. All things turned upside down when Heloise became pregnant and then they realized the hidden danger of remaining in France. They fled to Brittany the birth place of Abelard where Heloise gave birth to a boy whom they named Astrolabe.

The uncle of Heloise, Fulbert was furious and got Abelard castrated with the help of his servants while he was asleep. Abelard could not bear the ignominy and became a monk and dedicated his life to Philosophy and Theology. Heloise was forced by her uncle to give up her child for adoption and become a nun. However she remained in love with Abelard and they wrote many letters to each other during the rest of their life. Their heart-rending and affectionate love letters were published later on and continued to touch the hearts of thousands of people across the world. Although they could not unite during their life time the ill-fated lovers rest in eternal peace and tranquillity in the Pere Lachaise cemetery in Paris. Their tombs stand silently as symbols of medieval mystery of forbidden love and romance.

There is something mystique and mysterious about the love laden life of Abelard and Heloise, perhaps of all star-crossed tragic lovers of history. The story of Abelard and Heloise appealed to the young men and women of all times. Love is the commonest phenomenon which pervades the life of any human being made of flesh and blood. No one is exempted from the so-called weakness of the flesh although we pretend to be untouched by the temptation of the body. Even saints, sages, and seers are seen entangled in the rapturous motion of the emotion called love. The scandalous sexual life of many so-called god-men bears ample testimony to their dubious ways of life.

All love stories are similar. But some love stories are different from others in intensity, gravity and the tinge of divinity. The love story of Abelard and Heloise surpassed all love stories and romances of the world. It was a tragic saga of love, romance, tragedy, melodrama, social taboos, surreptitious relation, illicit child and final discomfiture. They could never live together as husband and wife and could not even talk for twelve years. But they cherished love in the recesses of their hearts. They made their love immortal through their emotion soaked letters which raised love to ecstatic heights. It was in the sad separation that their souls united in communion. Then the plenitude and profundity of their love once denied inflamed in them more than ever. No wonder the modern lovers who visit the cemetery where Abelard and Heloise were buried, leave love letters on the tomb.

It was perhaps fate or the trust of Heloise's uncle Fulbert in Abelard which resulted in the meeting of Abelard and Heloise. Fulbert was proud of his intellectual calibre of his niece and her proficiency in Latin, Greek and Hebrew languages. He wanted to have a scholar of eminence like Abelard to coach her as a home tutor. Thus Abelard got easy access to Heloise's house in 1114 A.D. when he was at the prime of his youth. That was the beginning of the most exciting but poignant love story of the world between a tutor in his thirties and a student in her teens. They passed time tutoring in love and romance. And as Abelard himself wrote in his memoirs, "more kissing than teaching" passed between them. They spent their available time in clandestine romance and inseparable meetings which evidently culminated in pregnancy and consequent discomfitures and humiliations.

There is an extraordinary brilliance and charm in the love of Abelard and Heloise. It is the love dalliance of two great intellectuals. Despite their differences in age and exposure to the world they had the fire of irresistible passion in them. Once their hearts got fire there was no escape from its consuming flames. All philosophies obfuscated, literature disappeared, logic became irrational and science became superstitious and the opponents appeared ruthless terminators. Robert Bridges said, "Love is a fire in whose devouring flame all earthly ills are consumed." Once Abelard and Heloise were consumed by the fire of passionate love all earthly things disappeared. Love was a kind of pleasant oblivion, a sad forgetfulness. Abelard's own words in one of his love letters are ponderable. He wrote "All men, I believe, are under a necessity of paying tribute at some time or other to love, and it is vain to avoid it. I was a philosopher and yet this tyrant of the mind trampled over all my wisdom; his darts were of greater force than all my reasoning and with a sweet restraint he led me wherever he pleased."

Abelard at one stage, exasperated by the painful separation offered to rectify the scandalous situation by a formal marriage. Fulbert also believed to have agreed to the proposal. But Heloise refused. She asserted that marriage and the responsibilities of a family could spoil the distinguished career of Abelard as a philosopher. According to her family life was incompatible with the work of a philosopher. Marriage may seem more sacred and binding but is purely an economic arrangement. Ironically she told that she would like to be called a mistress or a concubine or even a whore than fettering Abelard in conjugal relationship. This attitude was something incredible. But Heloise had an ardent devotion for Abelard and confessed that even during prayers her thoughts were disrupted by the imagination of carnal pleasures which she had once shared with Abelard. This frank admission shows how the waves of love permeated her very being and to which she surrendered herself. Abelard was in her thoughts and visions for ever that it was she who was responsible for making their love immortal.

The love story of Abelard and Heloise survived through their marvellous love letters. Abelard had depicted the details of their sweet and sour memories in his edifying autobiography Historia Calamitatum or **'The Story of my Misfortunes'** (circa 1132). The book provides his views on love and learning, monastic life and scholastic life, and rational and emotional life. It is an exceptionally honest self-portrait in the backdrop of his historic love affair with adorable Heloise. Abelard's detractors, people who conspired to denigrate him especially his intellectual rivals, like Bernard of Clairvaux caused him prolonged persecution. Bernard was a strict adherent of faith and Abelard's rationalism was depicted as desecration. He was arraigned for heresy at the ecclesiastical council of Sens in 1140. His enemies planned to secure condemnation of Abelard from the Pope. However unfortunately on his way to Rome Abelard collapsed physically and mentally and finally died in 1142 at the priory of St. Marcel.

The tomb of French lovers Heloise and Abelard in Père Lachaise Cemetery in Paris.

That was the tragic finale of a great intellectual whose love with Heloise rendered a transcendental and sublime dimension to love. Abelard the monk and Heloise the Abbess were bound to lead a sequestered life in their respective monastery and nunnery. It was during those years of alienation that they exchanged passionate love letters. The letters originally written in Latin are emotional remembrance of their lost love and the harrowing attempts to reconcile love with the monastic life and duty to remain chaste. They experienced tremendous crisis and tension between the two opposed poles of emotional and ecclesiastical life.

The story of Abelard and Heloise has the semblance of love affairs of all ages. There are such affairs even in the contemporary society. Teachers having love affair with students and vice versa are not uncommon even today. Even after one thousand years the love dalliance of Abelard and Heloise fascinates our imagination. The teacher and his student enter into a love liaison which was absolutely unacceptable to the society. They were not expected to take delight in the interdicted subject of 'teacher-taught' love and romance. Even today social norms, strictures and moral precepts do not accept such love affairs although legally they are permissible.

Abelard and Heloise however, set an ideal for the modern lovers that in love one must be intrepid and iconoclastic. Adjustment, acceptance and sacrifice are three primary conditions of love. Heloise sacrificed not just her earthly reputation as an intellectual but her heavenly salvation for the sake of secular love and romance.

The love of Abelard for Heloise was also based on unstinted sacrifice. He had to face a lot of mental tortures from his rivals. But he bore everything with great patience. Love was the religion of both the lovers. Even when they were wrapped in their monastic robes, the powerful love lurked in their hearts. They had been uncompromising on their unconventional ideas and convictions. The lovers of today must be inspired by their courage, defiance and glorification of Eros over morality. They are examples of dare-devil attitude to encounter the flames of hell for the sake of love and the carnal experience of love.

As for Heloise "Love has no business with law or money or social safety nets". We must appreciate her frankness, and sincerity in declaring the primacy of desire and amorous but sacrilegious motive of love. True love flourished even in adverse and unfavourable ambiences and among unexpected adversities and adversaries. The lovers must outright reject anything that opposes their love. Abelard said, "It is thousand times easier to renounce the world than love. I hate this deceitful faithless world. Think no more of it."

The love letters of Abelard and Heloise in fact testify the depth and intensity of their love. They were not simply romantic overflow of emotions of two lost lovers, but were deep philosophical letters. The letters contained the spirit of passion and erudition. Although Abelard wanted to distance himself from Heloise after his tragic experience Heloise encouraged him to remain committed to philosophy and his profession. Abelard on his part insisted that he had never truly loved her, but only lusted after her. He even expressed the feeling of guilt and said that their relationship was a sin against God. He told her to turn her love towards Jesus Christ and consecrate fully to religious vocation. Thus in the ultimate analysis they experience "pure love," the ascetic religious experience.

xxxxxxxxxxxxx

FIVE

MAD JOANNA AND HANDSOME PHILIP

THE STORY OF CRAZY PASSION

History abounds in absurd stories of abnormal and crazy lovers. We come across eccentric personalities in every country and in every culture. There were people of great position in the past who displayed extremely obnoxious psychic symptoms of love disorders. Kings and courtier, sergeants and powerful people nurtured erotic love and romance. Many a time they made their lives and the lives of others intolerably miserable by their bizarre behaviour. Rulers relinquished power, Kings neglected kingdoms, and able princes became damn drunkards and ultimately met their doom and disaster. There were also people with abnormal sexual desires involving dangerous activities in the past. Narcissism, sadism, masochism, lesbianism, homosexuality, paraphilia and similar abnormal activities were common among people with obsessive love. Thus sometimes love and romance became mad expressions of abnormal and selfish behaviour. Love got inevitably associated with sex and eroticism and changed everything contrary to the normal behaviour.

Catherine the great, Russian empress was described as a 'serial monogamist' because she had a number of lovers in her life. However her love for Gregory Potemkin was the love of her life. He was one of the several guards who overthrew her husband Peter III in a coup and installed her in power in 1762 A.D. She was notorious for her sexual promiscuity. She once said "The trouble is that my heart is loathed to remain even one hour without love". She loved to be loved! Edward VIII of British royal family had abdicated the throne to marry Wallis Simpson an American divorcee with two ex-husbands alive. Henry VIII king of England from 1509 to 1547 had contracted six marriages. His bedroom liaisons continued to show his penchant for exotic women. Ann Boleyn was Henry's second wife. She was charged with having sexual relationship with five courtiers due to her freak and avid carnal appetites. She had also conspired to kill her own husband, the king, and was however finally beheaded for treason.

Indian invader Alauddin Khilji's' obsession with beautiful Rani Padmini's mirror reflection had been an infamous episode of Indian history. Irish English poet William Butler Yeats' infatuation with the tall, slim and beautiful Maud Gonne did not materialize. Gonne married another man and had a daughter. After Gonne's separation from her husband McBride in 1916 Yeats again proposed to her. But she told him, "Marriage would be such a dull affair. Poets should never marry. The world should thank me for not marrying you". In utter desperation and confusion Yeats asked Gonne's daughter Iseult to marry him. She was 22 years old and considered Yeats' offer but ultimately Iseult refused to marry a man of her father's age.

Even Popes were not free from romantic and sexual advances. Pope John XII who became pope at the age of eighteen was a notorious sex fiend. Love meant carnal pleasures and sexual orgies. He was ultimately done away with while making love with a married woman. Pope Alexander VI married and sired many legitimate and a few illegitimate children outside of marriage in his licentious life. Pope Julius II reportedly had several mistresses and had been charged with lewd sexual acts. The love life of first century Roman emperor Nero surpassed all bizarre varieties of love.

Nero was the most notorious emperor who fiddled while Rome burnt in the great fire. He was so cruel that he killed his own mother Agrippina, his wives Octavia and Poppaca Sabina. He fell in love with Statilia Messalina a beautiful aristocratic lady. Nero had her fourth husband executed and made her his third wife. He was known for his most perverted love, sex and marriage.

There are many such exotic and bizarre varieties of love and romance in history.

There are also stories of men and women crippled by eccentric expression of love. One such fantastic story revolves around the fifteenth century royal couple Joanna 'the mad' and Philip 'the handsome'. Their love and married life read like a frightening horror story. Joanna was the daughter of Isabella of Castile and Ferdinand II of Aragon Spain. She was known with the epithet "the mad queen" of Castile (1479–1555) and was the mother of famous emperor Charles V. She was born at Burgos, a city of Spain, and grew like a child bereft of love amidst strange sounds and unfamiliar faces. Joanna was lonely and isolated. As a child she witnessed with horror hundreds of heretics being burnt alive. Although moody and restless she grew up to be a clever and intelligent girl. She was fond of reading and had command over French, Latin and Portuguese languages besides the skill in black arts. At the tender age of seventeen her parents decided to marry her to Philip the handsome of Austria, son of Roman emperor Maxmilian. The prince was so enamoured by the bewildering beauty of Joanna that raising a red wine glass he cried, "So delicate is the Lady Joanna's skin that were she to drink this red wine you could see it gliding down her throat!"

Joanna and Philip

Eighteen year old handsome Prince caught fire and a few months later they married. But unfortunately on the first night of marriage the hapless prince ran out of the bridal chamber pale and wild. Joanna refused to allow her marriage to be consummated. She did not heed to his repeated requests and frantic efforts to change her mind. Then he looked for consolation elsewhere and found it. Every night he visited passionate women to give vent to his suppressed feelings. He continued his philandering ways and his wife grew jealous to the point of depression and eventual lunacy. However Philip himself felt disgusted with the Spanish grandees and their suppressed smiles.

One night he secretly entered his wife's chamber with a drawn sword and demanded that she fulfill her marriage vows. He threatened to kill her, Joanna disrobed herself and bound a black cloth around her eyes and told, "If you care to take me thus you can satisfy both your wish and make good your threat!" Philip began to tremble and left the chamber. He refused food and drinks from that time and languished. Everybody blamed Joanna for the malady. Then one day Philip fell at Joanna's feet and wept and she surrendered to him. That night was marvellous and the whole palace was filled with music and merriment. Thereafter Joanna started loving Philip deeply. She was silent, ever present, and filled him with never ending love and affection. But Philip gradually started feeling the burden of excessive love and often returned to his nocturnal excursions secretly because he was afraid of his wife!

Meanwhile Joanna gave birth to a girl child. Her father feared return of her childhood peculiarities of violent behaviour. He kept the child away from her because of her unpredictable behaviour. Philip did not spend more time with Joanna. He was more at ease with his black-eyed Moorish country girls. Joanna knew that Philip deceived her but she tolerated everything and closed her eyes. However between 1498 and 1507 she gave birth to six children, Eleanor, Charles V, Isabella, Ferdinand, Mary and Catherine all of whom grew up to be emperors and queens.

Philip had many extramarital affairs. Joanna indulged in 'love potions' and super natural tricks to maintain her love for him. The increasing isolation from her husband made her mental breakdowns more and more severe. She also had to face power rivalry from all sides including her father, brother and husband. The frantic efforts of the paranoid Joanna could not bear the amorous propensities of Philip. Philip died in 1506 apparently due to fever but as rumours at galore he was poisoned at the instance of Joanna herself consequent upon a conspiracy. Ironically Philips' death made Joanna silent and strange with every passing day. She did not believe that Philip was dead. She opened his chests, took out his garments, and kissed his golden chains and rings.

Joanna at Philip's funeral

One day she went with her trusted servants to the cemetery where Philip was buried. She ordered the frightened monks to open the stone lid of the burial vault. She opened the coffin and made a sinister smile at Philip's face. Joanna prayed and it seemed to her disordered mind that God heard her prayers. And ignoring all protests of the monks she took the embalmed corpse to the palace. She dressed Philip's dead body in a splendid robe of silver and placed in a coffin of crystalline glass that could be opened at the top. She kept the coffin beside her bed and spent hours gazing at Philip's face. She let no woman enter the room. Joanna paid no attention to the threats and trepidations of the clergy who ordered the body to be restored to the tomb. She got an ingenious machine like an alarm clock and fitted to the body making a hole at the back. The ticking of the machine sounded like heartbeats and could be wound up for twenty four hours. Joanna would lie and listen to the sound of dead Philip's heart beat!

Joanna with the embalmed corpse of Philip

As days passed, pressure mounted on her to bury the body. Then she left Burgos with the body of Philip for which she hired a hundred stout highly paid foot soldiers known as lansquenets. She travelled months and months, from city to city, village to village and from castle to castle with the corpse. However in spite of her grisly burden she was welcomed at the castles of nobles. She paid valuable gifts and rewards for their hospitality. The coffin was taken in the form of a royal funeral procession and the mad queen herself rode directly behind the coffin. When the procession stopped to rest in an inn or castle she kept the coffin in her room. Joanna would then open the coffin and listen to the regular heart beat of the clock-heart like a child. She would embrace the body, whisper in its ears, kiss its pallid brow and would softly say. "Rest well, love and dream sweet dreams!"

At last one night while her fantastic cortege was passing through a snowy mountain pass, a snow slide carried away the coffin and the mules over the precipice. Joanna lost consciousness and lay on bed for weeks in a village. When she recovered and regained consciousness she had not asked anything about the coffin. The body of Philip was recovered from a snow filled hollow badly disfigured. Philips mortal remains were laid to rest in St. Andrew's church. Joanna spent the rest of her life surrounded by cats and was dead to feelings and emotions.

The story of handsome Philip and mad Joanna is heart rending. It is the saga of survival of two individuals despite their ostensible incompatibilities. Philip and Joanna hailed from reputed royal families. But unfortunately they could not live together for a long time. Philip died before he was not even thirty years and Joanna lived almost fifty more years after his death. Their marriage was not a happy one with a philandering husband and a paranoiac wife both struggling to overcome their own destiny. We feel sympathy for both and at the same time appreciate their consistency and commitment in love.

The devastating problem started on the very first night of wedding when the irresistible quest for conjugal consummation was thwarted by the bride herself. This astoundingly outlandish behaviour would have outright terminated the very marital relationship.

But ironically there was some positive note in the nuptial knot. We see the emergence of love between them although it did not last for long because of the sad and sudden death of Philip. However they raised six children Catharine being the last one posthumously born.

A very poignant factor in the love of Philip and Joanna was the mental disorder of Joanna. It aggravated in the form of extravagant jealousy towards other women close to unfaithful Philip. Joanna could not tolerate any other woman trespass into her exclusive domain of her husband's love for her. One day Joanna saw Philip flirting with a woman in the palace. Joanna started hacking of her rival's hair with a scissors. This act of violence did not mitigate her anger and Joanna stabbed the woman on her face. Such paranoiac behaviour was in her very personality. Ironically, the death or murder of Philip intensified her melancholia and depression, because of which she refused to be parted from the imbalanced body. Joanna presents the deadly horrendous face of love. Love is not always soft and appealing; it is sometimes hard and appalling. Many a time it is displayed in the extreme form of disgusting psychic disorder.

Six

CLEOPATRA AND ANTONY

THE VILE SERPENT OF NILE

The story of love, lust and infatuation of the first century B.C. lovers Antony and Cleopatra captivates anybody's imagination even today. Antony [83–30 B.C] was a brave Roman general and Roman Emperor Caesar's lieutenant and one of the second triumvirs and was in charge of the Eastern provinces. Cleopatra [69–30 B.C.] was the last queen of Macedonian dynasty of Egypt, established by Ptolemy, the general of Alexander the Great, after her father's death in 51 B.C. Their love dalliance is extremely enticing because of Cleopatra rather than the lost lover Antony. Cleopatra the beautiful queen of Egypt had been the inspiration of poets, romancers, novelists and playwrights of all ages including Shakespeare and Bernard Shaw. She was a fascinating and attractive woman. She was made of such stuff as men would never forget. Shakespeare extols Cleopatra in the following words in the play Antony and Cleopatra.

"Age cannot whither her, nor custom stale

Her infinite variety".

These words depict her youthful ebullience, fascinating unpredictability and range of mood. She had all the feminine attributes to enrapture even an astute ascetic not to mention of an ordinary mortal. Cleopatra was delighted to live the life of pleasure and profligacy. The kingdom of Egypt and its wealth existed only for her love and reckless lust. Handsome, sturdy and strong men were only objects of the amorous advances of her royal life. They distracted her and she let them love her when she was bored and was despondent. She cherished the feeling of superiority of her beauty and power of attraction. Her motto was, "Why am I beautiful if not to be loved?"

She flirted and flitted from one man to another like a butterfly which hovered in a flower garden and passed from passion to passion. When love began to bore, Cleopatra had her hapless lovers flung to the crocodiles or given the poison cup. It is not because she was cruel and barbaric but because the victims had completed their role! Egypt was full of love stuff should boredom befell on her. Many a time feminine ploys and tantrums dominated her behaviour. She wanted to find out the whereabouts of Antony and tells the maid-

'If you find him sad,
Say I am dancing;
If in mirth report that
I am sudden sick."

Anthony and Cleopatra

Cleopatra was not an ordinary woman and like a serpent she coiled men in her ensnaring traps. Men never forgot her but she forgot them as soon as she was wearied of them. She could transform anyone who came into contact with her. Antony was called the

'Strumpet's fool' because of his transformation after his infatuation with Cleopatra.

The crafty Cleopatra, already married lost no opportunity to win over Julius Caesar before Antony. She went to the palace in Alexandria where Caesar was staying accompanied by only one attendant. She wrapped herself in a golden carpet to avoid resistance from her incestuous brother Ptolemy XIII. Caesar was overwhelmed by the charm of Cleopatra and soon two became allies in politics and lovers in life. A son was born in their royal alliance in 47 BC and was named Caesarion. Cleopatra visited Rome after one year with her love child. But she had to flee Rome after Caesar was stabbed to death in the Roman Senate. The Roman people, however, loved Cleopatra's exotic hairstyle and fashionable jewellery and many Roman women adopted the 'Cleopatra look'.

Cleopatra

Cleopatra's deep love dalliance with Mark Antony radically transformed the life of both. Their love and romance developed into a tragic saga of epic dimension and fascinated the whole world. It was a story of the 'immortal longings' of Cleopatra and the irresistible infatuation of Antony. The legendary love story was spectacular and exquisitely enduring. Antony had all the attributes to attract the fastidious Cleopatra. He was handsome, mirthful, lustful, boisterous and moody. He was also very liberal and popular with his men. It is said that Antony's heart fluttered whenever he saw a skirt!

Antony had met Cleopatra as the young mistress of his mentor Caesar in Rome. The seeds of infatuation were sown at that time and after Caesar's assassination Antony was made in charge of Roman Empire's rowdy eastern territories. The safety and security of the vast eastern exploits needed a brave man like the indomitable Antony. In 41 BC while Antony was staying in the city of Tarsus near the Turkish coast he sent for Cleopatra. She was aware of Antony's brewing infatuation for her and made a stunning royal appearance before him. The moment Antony saw her he lost his head and virtually fell flat in love. Thereafter it was a decade of flirting, romance and display of splendour and elegance. Their attraction appeared genuine but had ulterior motives for both. Antony needed rich and ambitious Cleopatra to fund his eastern military expeditions and Cleopatra needed protection to expand her power and assert the rights of her son Caesarion.

Antony followed Cleopatra to Alexandria and the two powerful rulers lived an exuberant life of fun and frolic, banquets and soirees, dancing and drinking. It was altogether a lascivious and lustful life of extravagance, profligacy and carefree enjoyment. Meanwhile she gave birth to their twins named Alexander Helios and Cleopatra Selene. Antony went back to Rome to report on his eastern triumphs. There he married Octavia, the sister of Octavian. Antony and Cleopatra did not meet for three years but were reunited in 37 BC and started life where they last ended.

It was during this period that Antony started facing setbacks. He managed everything in confusion and was under the influence of certain drugs and devastating looks of Cleopatra. He was not the master of his own faculties. Antony's passion for Cleopatra was intense and unfaltering. Cleopatra was over-possessive in her love for Antony. His enchantment with the queen was such that there was absolute disregard for everything other than the bewitching beauty of Cleopatra. She had a jealous suspicion about Antony's love and loyalty toward her especially in comparison with his Roman wife Fulvia. To remove all doubts Antony replied,

"Let Rome in Tiber melt,

And the wide arch

Of the ranged empire fall.

Here is my space."

Mark Antony was revelling his time in Egypt, living a life of decadence when he got the news of his wife Fulvia's death and Pompey's rebellion against the triumvirs. Antony's companions of the triumvirs

Lepidus and Caesar Octavius, Julius Caesar's grand nephew, condemned him for neglecting his duties as a statesman. Antony returned to Rome in order to confirm and consolidate his loyalty to Rome. There Antony married Caesar's sister Octavia. However nothing could mend their solidarity. A series of battles were fought between Antony and Caesar culminating in the suicide of Antony. The victorious Caesar planned to display the Egyptian queen in Rome as a testament to the might of his empire. Cleopatra knew about his insidious plan and committed suicide by self-inflicting stings of Asp, a poisonous snake. Both the lovers were buried side by side in Alexandria in a splendid and regal fashion.

The romantic love that flourished in the land of Pharaohs and pyramids between Antony and Cleopatra was the communion of two countries, two cultures and two civilizations, the Roman and the Egyptian. Shakespeare depicted the first century romance in his play Antony and Cleopatra with splendid romantic colours. It was he who acquainted the world with the "infinite variety" of Cleopatra. Like Romeo and Juliet it is a marvellous romantic tragedy. In Romeo and Juliet the ultimate death of two star-crossed lovers reconciled two feuding families. But the suicide of two lovers, Antony and Cleopatra could not create any rapport between Rome and Egypt. After Antony's death even all his statues were pulled down, according to Plutarch, but those of Cleopatra were left untouched on request of Caesar's friend Archibius, for which he paid 200 talents to Caesar.

It is impossible to define the prismatic love and lust of Antony and Cleopatra through normal norms of ethics and morality. We have to identify the impulsive features of love in them as individuals. Antony was a brave Roman warrior and a powerful statesman, the most efficient of the triumvirs. But unfortunately he was intoxicated in infatuation of Cleopatra. He was a married man, lost himself completely to the captivating beauty of Cleopatra who had a dubious past in love, and marriage. His first marriage was with Fadia, followed by Antonia, Hybrida Minor, Fulvia, Octavia and Cleopatra. They bore him children and nothing much is known about them except one or two who later on adorned the throne. His love and romance with his paramour resulted in utter neglect of the royal family as well as the royal kingdoms and possessions.

Antony's love was a kind of surrender to the serpentine beauty of the splendorous queen. He lost his personal gravity and belligerent spirit when he was with Cleopatra. She on her part played a thousand and one amorous advances to attract Antony's attention and captivated him in the magic aura of her infinite variety. Plutarch wrote, "Plato admits four sorts of Flattery, but Cleopatra had a thousand." She played dice with him, drank with him, and hunted with him and sometimes maintained sulky silence with him.

Antony was inescapably caught in the love trap of Cleopatra. We can guess the desperation and discomfiture of Antony and his extreme sense of dejection and resignation in the words, "O, whither hast thou led me, Egypt?" Antony considered his ways just and noble and never minded the decadence of the state. Initially Antony came to Egypt to consolidate Rome's eastern exploits and expand the empire with the support of the queen who had a huge treasure of jewels, pearls, gems and gold. But wealth apart he wedded the wealthy queen's heart and her political domain.

Cleopatra's love was indescribable, indefinable and multifaceted. She stood on the dubious borderline of lover, wife, prostitute, paramour, whore, harlot, seducer, concubine, cocotte, enchantress or a Bella Donna. It is difficult rather impossible to assign a name to her love. She carried traits of all in one. She was a married woman, a promiscuous lady who led a lascivious life of love, lust and sex with strong athletic and handsome men. Love for her was an incestuous experience as prevalent in the Ptolemaic tradition to maintain purity of blood lineage. Cleopatra married both her adolescent brothers but eliminated them in collusion with Julius Caesar to take possession of the throne.

Cleopatra was a debauched enchantress who used sex appeal as a political weapon to capture power and to stay in power. She used this trait of her love, to entice Caesar and Antony. Like the Greek beauty Helen she had the power to captivate the most powerful men like Caesar and Antony. She was not a dullard lover but very pragmatic and a utilitarian as far as her interests were concerned. She was an expert in the art of entrancing her potential allies. She wrapped herself in a carpet when she went to meet Caesar. She made up to look like goddess Aphrodite when she went to meet Antony who considered himself the embodiment of the Greek god Dionysus.

Cleopatra's love for Antony had a soft and delicate dimension also despite the apparent complexity and hardness. Love was a sensual, tender and tenuous feeling and also a passionate and attractive sensation. She was adept in the conjuring art of wooing, cajoling, and pampering the sentiments of men. She talks about Antony's wife, "Fulvia is perchance angry with you". "Why did you marry Fulvia?" etc. to coax Antony and make him friendly.

She used her sex appeal and bewitching looks and pampering tricks to ensnare Antony and make him a slave of love and lust for ever. She asked Antony "If it be love indeed tell me how much", to which Antony replied metaphorically, "There is beggary in the love that can be reckoned", meaning that the depth and intensity of his love cannot be measured. Once within the ensnaring allurements of Cleopatra Antony was unable to move out of the mesmerizing beauty of Cleopatra. No wonder on seeing the dead body of Cleopatra, Caesar remarked,

"She looks like sleep
As she would catch another Antony
In her strong toil of grace"

(Antony and Cleopatra)

The love of Antony and Cleopatra was not simply the innocent Platonic love but intentional erotic, sexual love which made Antony the inevitable victim of sexual profligacy. Antony found himself inescapably entangled in the ravishing charm of Cleopatra. However in spite of the apparent sensuality of love Cleopatra cherished a desire and willingness to motherhood. Normally the socialite women refrain from pregnancy and raising children due to the fear and anxiety over disfigurement and loss of physical attraction. As for Cleopatra children were essential to retain and safeguard her kingdom. She had four small thrones to seat her children near the royal throne. She ensured the future of her four children Selene, Helios and Philia Delphos with Antony and Caesarion with Julius Caesar. However none of them could survive the aftermath of the decisive battle of Actium in 31 BC and the tragic death of their parents.

There is nothing profoundly divine and mystical about the love and romance of Antony and Cleopatra. It was simply insatiable erotic excitements. Love was depicted as the conjugal alliance between incestuous Cleopatra and polygamous Antony. Their love was flamboyant and peripheral. It had all dimensions except depth and its foundation was nothing but personal interests and convolutions of political power.

Antony was an infatuated lover ensnared by voluptuous Cleopatra's external beauty and sexual appeal. Her love was based on the principles of profit and loss unlike the love of many Shakespearean heroines like Juliet, Desdemona, Miranda, Ophelia etc. She was not sincere in her love for any single man but loved all men who were unassailable in power and attraction in physique and appearance. She gave the impression to each lover that he was her ultimate heart-throb. She displayed it in her possessive behaviour and little acts of anger and annoyance. She expected her enamoured consort to pamper and appease her because she knew men are basically fools and slaves of the stunning beauty of women.

xxxxxxxxxxxxx

Seven

KING RODERICK AND FLORINDA

THE SAD SPANISH LOVE STORY

The early 8th century A.D. was a dark period in the history of ancient Spain ruled by the Gothic kings of Germanic origin. This tragic period became infamous due to the legendary love story of king Roderick and Florinda. It was not in fact a romantic love in the strict conventional sense. It was a tale of one-sided romance and infatuation, treachery and sexual outrages. Sincere romance is the exquisite fascination and attraction for the opposite sex. However, in the case of Roderick and Florinda it started with the fear and anxiety of the unfortunate and hapless girl. This devastating Spanish love story was a gross betrayal of trust and humanity.

The poor girl Florinda in her immature teens was the tragic victim of royal intemperance and sexual passions. The legend does not excite our imagination because the girl as a vulnerable victim. It was perhaps a case of forcible love affair, love that was not emotionally reciprocated. However the love story fascinated the people of Spain because it was intimately connected to their history and culture. The writers of successive generations like Robert Southey, Walter Scott and historians immortalized the legend through their memorable writings.

The story of the illicit love of king Roderick for an innocent girl was responsible for the unprecedented political upheaval in Spain and its conquest by the Moors. Roderick was the last prominent king of the Visigoths who ruled Spain for a very short period from 710 to 712 A.D. He acquired power through a violent palace coup which ended in the assassination of the legitimate king Wittiza. After seizing power Roderick ruled from the city of Toledo. Roderick probably got the support of the senate which consisted of the aristocrats and even bishops. Like all usurpers of power Roderick was murdered in his early twenties in the war with the armies of Arabs and Muslims. His widow Egilona married the first Muslim governor of Hispania.

Conquest of Spain by the Muslim Army

King Roderick had a powerful and trusted companion named Count Julian who was the governor of Ceuta, an autonomous Spanish territory on the African coast. He used to gift Roderick horses, hawks and many valuable productions of foreign countries. Count Julian had a beautiful daughter named Florinda. Roderick entrusted Julian with the onerous duty of his African military expeditions. After the death of her mother the king himself volunteered to be the royal guardian of Florinda when Julian was away on his army operations. There were many beautiful girls as maids to the queen Egilona. The lustful king had his vulture's eyes on the sixteen year old innocent daughter of Julian who had confidently confided his daughter to the care of his trusted friend and mentor.

Count Julian was a great courageous commander and a fearless warrior. But he was mistaken in judging the malicious intention of his royal mentor. He expected a bright future for the motherless child when he remained away from home in the battlefield. The concupiscent king frequently followed the innocent girl with bad intentions. One day it so happened that a group of maids of the queen including beautiful Florinda were sporting in the palace garden. The innocent merry-making girls in great fun and frolic wanted to display the bewitching beauty of Florinda as superior to another girl who was the black beauty named Zora.

The girls in a noisy rollicking mood disrobed the delicately clothed Florinda. To the utter misfortune of the poor girl the ravenous eyes of the king fell on her delicate body from the palace Alcazar. His greedy eyes saw the uncovered body of the girl and surveyed her captivating gestures. That unlucky moment proved disastrous and devastating not only for Florinda but also for the whole Spanish kingdom.

King Roderick had virtually become a captive of the forbidden charm of Florinda. He could not forget the bewildering and enchanting beauty of the girl. The beautiful maid made him mad with passion and fascination for her. He patiently waited for an opportunity to have a glimpse of her and to converse with her in solitude. He was enamoured by the unforgettable looks and mesmerizing beauty of Florinda.

One day the wily king with his wicked intention met the poor girl in a solitary corner of the palace. He gently approached the unwary girl apparently with a paternal tenderness and gently told her "Dear, there is a thorn in your hand." The king then volunteered to remove the imaginary thorn. The poor girl with a reverential feeling towards the fatherly man offered her hand to the wicked king to remove the non-existent thorn. The unsuspecting girl innocently told the king "Your Majesty, there is no thorn." The frightened Florinda understood something fishy and swiftly retreated to escape from the bad behaviour of the king. However the king already burning with passion pressed the hand of the helpless girl to his rough and strong chest and told "Darling, the thorn is here."

The king's passionate gestures were disgusting and extremely unpleasant to Florinda. She looked reproachfully at the fatherly figure standing in front of her. She was embarrassed and confused at the unexpected situation. It was unbelievable for an innocent girl like Florinda. She realized some impending danger hidden in the unnatural behaviour of the king. She had never in her life faced such uncomfortable behaviour from anyone which caused fear and apprehension in her. At last Florinda mustered courage and told the king with despise "My father told me you are like my father."

Roderick was upset and annoyed at the girl's words of refusal. He felt dishonoured because of the reticence and resistance of the girl. The words of simplicity and ignorance of Florinda at the imperial gesture angered the king. Nothing annoyed a heart filled with passion more than a girl's reluctance due to inexperience. The king tried to entice Florinda by offering her all the pleasures of the palace. He told her that he would not degrade her to the level of a common girl. He tried to attract her through many allurements. However nothing could deter her from her attitude towards the king. Florinda understood that the demand of the king was beyond her virtuous life and that he was bent upon to spoil her purity. She expressed her suppressed feeling with great indignation. Finally she cried "I would rather die than submitting to dishonour."

Florinda tried to escape from the passionate clutches of the lusty king. The frail unlucky girl could not resist the powerful hold of the king. She was brutally raped. Florinda could not protect her honour from the threats and compulsions of the lecherous predator. The king was adept and experienced in the art and techniques of seducing women. There was nothing immoral and indecent in love and romance in the opinion of the king. The cries and desperate entreaties of the hapless girl fell into deaf ears. The king felt no scruple or compunction on his act of sexual atrocity. Roderick thought that Florinda would be afraid of divulging his misdemeanour and sexual assault on her.

However, Florinda could not forgive the man for his gluttonous acts because she adored Roderick as a father figure. Florinda could not forget the emotional wounds that he inflicted on her delicate mind. One day she decided to reveal everything to her father who had entrusted her to the care of his friend with great expectation. Florinda wrote a despairing letter to her father Julian. The words were touching. She wrote "Alas! My father, you entrusted your lamb to a wolf! The king who should have been a father to me has abused and dishonoured me. Take me from this polluted court to some quiet convent where I can hide my shame until death releases me from suffering. Come quickly to your unhappy child."

The painful missive was enough to wrench the heart of any father. Count Julian was terribly angry at the audacious act of betrayal of his intimate friend. His heart was filled with hatred and detestation of the man whom he wholeheartedly trusted. Julian returned to Toledo and without expressing anything about what had happened in the royal palace took away his daughter to Ceuta. He knew that if the king got any inkling of the letter the consequence would be fatal to him and his daughter. He therefore nurtured secret vengeance in his heart and waited for the opportune time to strike.

Julian could not forgive and forget the shameful act of outrage against the modesty and purity of his daughter. He, therefore, hatched a conspiracy with the Muslim ruler Musa to avenge the dishonour of his daughter from the king. Julian decided to undermine the throne of Roderick and disturb his dominion until it is completely annihilated.

There were many stories and legends about the Roderick and Florinda affair. One such legend described their love as genuine and reciprocal. According to it Roderick and Julian were good friends. One day Count Julian visited king Roderick at Toledo. He was accompanied by his servants and soldiers and his beautiful daughter Florinda. Julian entrusted his daughter to the kingly care of his trusted friend dreaming a bright future for her. Julian left the palace feeling complacent about his daughter's future.

Days passed and Florinda lived with the other maids of the queen. Then one day the inevitable happened. The king chanced upon Florinda bathing in the river. Roderick saw the creamy naked body of Florinda from the palace. He was fascinated and enamoured by her beauty and fell in love with her at the very first sight. Florinda also reportedly reciprocated to the amorous advances of the king without any compulsion.

There was yet another legend according to which Roderick knew about the very beautiful daughter of Count Julian. He told Julian that a damsel of virtue and repute must be under the care of the Queen Egilona which will enhance her prospects of marriage. Julian was happy at the royal offer and without hesitation sent his daughter to the court of Toledo. Florinda was received with great honour and was admitted among the noble damsels of the queen.

The king was enticed by the stunning beauty of Florinda and seduced her and she surrendered to his persistent advances. She succumbed willingly to Roderick's persuasive words, his professions of love and promises of future. Florinda shared her intimate secrets with her close friend Alquifa and revealed the details of her dishonour. Alquifa admonished her about the danger of getting pregnant. She advised her to write to her father about the affair. She urged her father to retrieve her from the court before the secret became public. Julian came immediately and took away his daughter with a stern determination to take revenge on the king for the betrayal.

Julian was infuriated by the royal breach of trust. He decided to teach Roderick a lesson. He colluded with the African Moors and betrayed Spain and the Visigoth ruler Roderick. In short the affair of Florinda and the determination of Julian and the ambition of the African Moors together led to the attack on Spain. Thus the Muslim occupation of the Spanish land continued for about 800 years.

The Goths and the Moors engaged in a fierce encounter on the bank of river Guadelete in 711 A.D. The war would never have been fought had not the king Roderick under uncontrolled passion deflowered the innocent girl Florinda. Her father Julian was bent on wrecking vengeance on the king who betrayed his trust. So for his personal revenge Julian took the support of ambitious Moors and betrayed Spain. The Spanish army was led by Roderick and the invading Muslim forces were commanded by powerful warrior

Tariq bin Ziyyad Amidst the terrible battle of revenge a group of soldiers led by Archbishop Oppas, Count Julian's brother-in-law, passed over to the enemy camp. Roderick threw off his helmet to display his identity unaware of the desertion in his army camp.

The Gothic soldiers ran helter skelter in panic and confusion and melted away in mad flight throwing away their swords, spears and battle axes. The Muslim army took advantage of the disarray and hundreds of Gothic men were slaughtered by the pursuing Muslim cavalry. King Roderick in exasperation turned to his profusely bleeding faithful charger Orelia and fled away from the battle field. While fleeing he could hear the shouts of victory of the enemies. Roderick perished in the battle and the invaders caused heavy destruction and havoc in Spain. Roderick's widow Egilona married the son of Arab army commander Musa Ibn Nusair named Abd al Aziz.

According to one legend Roderick lost everything and was totally devastated. The Spanish ballads depict the lament of king Roderick very touchingly in the following words,

"Last night I was the king of Spain, today no king am I,

Last night fair castles held my train,
tonight where shall I lie?
Last night a hundred pages
did serve me on the knee,
Tonight not one I call my own;
not one pertains to me."

The desperate Roderick went to a hermitage in search of peace of mind and tranquillity. The wise hermit asked the guilt stricken king to repent for his sins. The hermit led him to an open grave in which lay a big black snake. He told Roderick to stay with the snake in the grave to prove his repentance. If he truly repented for his wrong to the innocent Florinda the serpent would not harm him. On the contrary if he did not repent sincerely the serpent would not spare him. For two days the gnarling serpent did not harm Roderick. The third day Roderick's mind went astray from remorse. His thoughts roamed in the beautiful palace gardens. The bewitching beauty of Florinda captured his imagination. He re-lived the passionate moments of carnal pleasure he had enjoyed with enamouring Florinda.

Then the inevitable happened. The hermit heard a doleful voice emerging from the open grave. It was the distress voice of Roderick. He cried to the hermit "Father, the snake gnaws me! His teeth are destroying me where I most sinned!" After a terrible cry of pain and anguish there was sepulchral silence. King Roderick was dead! Julian who had betrayed his native land became the king of Spain and was powerful among the Moors. Florinda turned against her father in horror. She told him "All I asked was to be taken to a convent where I could mourn and pray. But instead you have given our land into the hands of the Muslims and my name is cursed by every Christian lip."

Florinda did not live long after the disastrous battle which led to the annexation of Spain by the Arab and Muslim invaders. The Spanish people blamed Florinda for the misfortune that fell on Spain. The called her 'La Cava' which meant 'The Harlot'. She was depicted as the Eve of Spain who was responsible for the decline, fall and desecration of Spain.

Florinda had to bear the pain and stigma of Roderick's sin. The thoughts and visions of Gothic warriors who sacrificed their lives for Spain tormented her mind. In utter despair she ended her life by flinging herself from the tower of her father's palace, the great Alcazar of Cordova.

The disaster of Spain was due to the attack of the Muslim invaders after the seduction of Julian's daughter Florinda. The inscrutable destiny also played its role in accelerating the fall of Spain. According to legend the city of Toledo was founded by Hercules. He built a tower to store treasure. There was an inscription on the heavy door of the tower which read "King of Spain if you open these doors, on your head be it." All the kings took the message seriously and added a new lock to the old locks. Gradually, as time passed adding a lock to the door became part of the royal coronation ceremony.

The covetous Roderick on becoming king, instead of adding a lock removed all the previous locks. He entered the tower and to his utter surprise found no treasure. He found in the empty tower an enormous painting which depicted the occupants of the royal castle fleeing from an invading army. There were also the abandoned flag and coat of arms of Spain. The king was shocked at the disturbing sight and prohibited others from entering the tower. The king regularly visited the tower and it was during those days that Julian came to the palace with his charming daughter.

The legend around king Roderick, his friend Count Julian and Julian's daughter La Cava Florinda dominated the history of Hispania during the medieval centuries. The tragic affair of Roderick with Florinda for his sexual gratification led to the great betrayal and consequent Muslim conquest and downfall of Spain. The stories and legends crystallized around the Spanish episode and innumerable romances and ballads were written on the theme. They began as anonymous poems which were transmitted orally in the recitations of the minstrels.

The brief period of reign of Roderick in Spain was full of exciting events and legends which had always been a fascination for poets and writers of all ages. The myths and legends of Roderick and Florinda enriched Spanish literature. Many writers of other countries and languages adopted the legends of romance, seduction and treachery in their writings, especially in novels and epic poems. Robert Southey depicted the character of Roderick with open-minded sympathy and compassion in his famous epic poem **Roderick, the Last of the Goths** composed in 1814. At the end of the epic Count Julian was assassinated by his own allies and the Moorish army was broken and defeated. The epic narration ended with the retreat of the vanquished king Roderick to the wilderness.

Roderick is the central figure in the English playwright William Cowley's tragedy **All's Lost by Lust** [1633]. The play depicted Roderick as a rapist who was dethroned by Count Julian and the Moors. The Scottish writer Walter Scott in his work **The Vision of Don Roderick [1811]** and the English writer Walter Savage Landor in his tragedy **Count Julian** [1812] handled the theme of the legend with marvellous skilfulness and perfection. The American author Washington Irving re-narrated the legends in his book **Legends of the Conquest of Spain** [1835]. There were also many operas and ballads related to the fabulous stories and legends of the Spanish fiasco.

The tragic alliance of Roderick and Florinda, whether true or false, historical or imaginary, was responsible for the epochal political change in Spain twelve centuries ago. It precipitated in the entry of the Islamic religion and culture in the cultural fabric of Spain. Had it not been for the atrocity and injustice of Roderick towards Florinda, there would have been no conspiracy between Julian and the Moors. The support of the insiders resulted in the Arab-Muslim invasion which caused the Spanish catastrophe and devastation.

Eight

THREE INSPIRING LOVE STORIES

The three legendary love stories narrated below are exceptional because they inspire the readers and transport them to a very different level of romantic love. They are wonderful tales of individuals for whom love is not simply effusions of passions. Love is a transcendent emotion, a kind of divine communion of two souls. In the legend of William Booth and Catherine Mumford love was a vocation which evinced honour, worship and adoration for an amiable person. Physical challenges did not deter them from their determination to marry although both of them were engaged in pastoral services. Their love was the fulfilment of their mission and passion for divine love, the love beyond the fickle and ludicrous world.

The passionate love between two great poets, Robert Browning and Elizabeth Barrett was rooted in mutual appreciation and evaluation of each other as writers. They had to face many hurdles in their love because of their difference in age, Barrett's physical challenges, and above all the objection of her adamant father to the alliance. However they were determined and boldly faced the strong oppositions from the orthodox society defiantly. The taught the lovers a marvellous lesson to love someone not for what he or she is, but for what you are when you are with him or her. Hence their love despite serious illness and marriage despite objections survived because of their strong courage of convictions and commitments. Love is a perpetual union of souls to melt into the ineffable Ultimate.

The fabulous love story of Dante and Beatrice is rather imaginative than a realistic It is symbolic of boundless and eternal love. It is spiritually charged with emotion which represents divinity. There is no sensualism in Dante's love for Beatrice. There is deep romantic radiance. Beatrice was in fact Dante's inspiration for his magnum opus The Diving Comedy, and a very beautiful work The New Life which depicted Dante's tragic love for Beatrice.

The three spectacular love legends depict different levels of passionate love.

(I) WILLIAM BOOTH AND CATHERINE MUMFORD

The marvellous love and marriage of William Booth (1829–1912) and Catherine Mumford (1829–1890) was similar to that of Robert Browning and Elizabeth Barrett. We have the image of William Booth as a long bearded, hoary headed venerable old man, a Christian minister and the founder of the world-wide Christian organization known as the Salvation Army devoted to evangelism and social work among the poorest and the most wretched people. There is, nevertheless, another image of William Booth, the youth of 22 years passionately in love with the young and ebullient Catherine Mumford. It was an instantaneous love at first sight impressing their minds with the feeling of made for each other. They recorded their valuable love moments and feelings through innumerable letters. William Booth realized that he was passionately and desperately in love with Catherine and cannot retrieve his steps.

William Booth and Catherine Mumford

Initially he thought his love to be some form of platonic friendship, a kind of ideological adoration of an amiable person. But gradually things slipped out of his control. He wrote "I honour you, I worship, I adore, I have loved' you, oh! Perhaps more than....." Then suddenly he realized "I am rambling on to forbidden ground." Catherine was aware of the vocation of William to be the minister of God and solicited him to forget her because the memory of their love would disturb his peace of mind.

However gradually she also felt the pleasant feeling of romantic attraction for him. She could not bear the brunt of even an imaginary disavowal of love and said "Oh! That we have never seen each other." In short both of them were in love, an inevitable predicament which they themselves had to resolve. Ultimately in May 1855 both married and committed themselves to Almighty God. They had a wonderful lifelong married life. They lived magnificently in communion and companionship in their inseparable spiritual love and understanding.

William Booth's beloved Catherine Mumford was an extraordinary woman with a firm conviction and clear views on issues like abstinence from alcohol, vegetarianism, problems related to girls and weaker sections of the society. She was a strong advocate of equality of women with men in the society. She can be considered as the forerunner of modern women's liberation movements and feminism. She opposed vehemently the traditional Victorian society which restricted the life of women to the four walls of the house, to cooking, washing, sweeping and raising children.

The childhood of Catherine was confined to bed because she suffered from acute spine, lungs and heart problems. Her father was a preacher and mother, a devout Methodist. They educated her at home and encouraged her to read the Bible, books on theology and church history. She read the whole Bible eight times before she was twelve years old, an incredible achievement for a chronically sick girl! She was an ideal woman committed to her family of eight children and at the same time helped her husband in his missionary activities. Catherine objected to the social, intellectual and moral inferiority of women in the society. She challenged the social taboos herself and took up preaching and proselytizing together with William from 1860. She died in 1890. Catherine had become so popular during her life span of six decades that her funeral was attended by thousands of people.

There is nothing unusual and abnormal about the love of two people engaged devotedly in pastoral services. But what bewilders anyone is the apparent incongruity in physical conditions. Catherine had many physical challenges and spent her fascinating adolescence in encountering those challenges. However, she had a tremendous will power to struggle and survive despite her personal problems. She fought against social evils and stood strongly in her faith. What fascinates anyone is that their love never appeared scandalous and objectionable even to the relatives. Their love was indeed the fulfilment of their mission and passion for divine love, the love beyond the ludicrous world.

We witness a rare communion of two souls ardently promoting the cause of religious faith and social equity. It was a splendid life of partnership and participation based on divine love, respect, trust and a very luminous disposition. They proved that love and marriage are divine endowments to execute the mission of life. Aristotle said, "Love is composed of a single soul inhabiting two bodies". The love of William and Catherine was sublimated and spiritualized like the luminous love of Dante and Beatrice which culminated in the glorification of love in the famous epic **'La Divina Commedia': The Divine Comedy**. The love of William and Catherine consummated in the foundation of the marvellous institution called the Salvation Army actively engaged in charitable and humanitarian works in more than 130 countries of the world.

(II) DANTE AND BEARTRICE

The thirteenth century story of Dante and Beatrice had a similar spiritual dimension of love. It was a fascination beyond fickleness of imagination. It was adoration without egoism. The spiritualism of Dante-Beatrice love was re-established in the evangelism of William Booth and Catherine Mumfield after almost five centuries. The spirit of real love appears in different forms in different ages. Dante Alighieri (1265–1321) was an Italian Poet and moral philosopher known for his epic poem 'The Divine Comedy', depicting the heaven, hell and purgatory, the three levels of after-life according to Christian theology. Although a married man Dante was irresistibly in love with another woman Beatrice Portinari (1265–1290) who made huge influence on Dante. Her character was the central theme of Dante's **Divine Comedy** and **The New Life** which depicted Dante's tragic love for Beatrice.

Historians dispute the actual identity of Beatrice of real life and the Beatrice of Dante's poetic creation. However Dante is said to have met the real Beatrice two or three times in their life time. But he immortalized the girl in his poems. Beatrice represented the divine light. She led Dante in his journey in the paradise through the nine levels of heaven and finally the empyrean region where God resided. Love is the guiding light of a man's spiritual of journey.

Dante and Beatrice

Dante's love for Beatrice was divine and symbolized spiritual radiance. It was unconditional, unchanging and boundless. She was his source of inspiration and even after her death he continued to love her because-

"She has ineffable courtesy, is my beatitude,
The destroyer of all vices
And the queen of virtue, salvation."

Beatrice was his spiritual guide in his heavenly itinerary. The inscrutable aspect of Dante's love for Beatrice was his virtual infatuation with her even in her absence. Dante, in fact created her as the incarnation of purity and immaculateness. There was no element of erotic sexuality and carnal inclination in their love.

After her death at a very young age of 25 years, Dante started composing poetry dedicated to her memory. He admired her beauty and goodness in The New Life. But he wanted to write something exclusive about his beloved which he fulfilled in the epic The Divine Comedy. She was his intimate companion and guide in his spiritual voyage. She appeared before Dante first time in the journey in the purgatory. Dante was overwhelmed by her sight as she was when he met her at the age of nine. Dante was dazed by her intimate companionship throughout the journey until she ascended to her place in heaven closest to God. This is absolute absorption of the two lovers into the divine blissfulness. Their love was the spiritualized love and the culmination of the pilgrimage. Beatrice, in essence, was the representation, the symbol of ideal beauty and grace.

Dante personified love through Beatrice who descended from heaven and asked Virgil to guide Dante through hell. Beatrice said,

"I come from where I most long to return;
Love prompted me,
That love which makes me speak".

The New Life depicted Dante's dream. A mighty figure appeared and said 'I am your Lord' (Ego Dominus tuus). The figure carried Beatrice in its arms and made her eat Dante's burning heart. Thus for Dante 'She was his beatitude, the destroyer of all vices, and the queen of virtues, salvation! He saw her as his saviour, the one who eradicated all evils from him. So love is for the purification of the mind, and ultimate salvation and communion with the almighty God. Beatrice was Dante's ideal of love rather than a physical form. Dante's courtly love just like the medieval concept of love was hidden and unrequited. It was a highly respectful form of admiration. That was the cause of immortality and perpetuity of the love of Dante and Beatrice.

(III) ROBERT BROWNING-ELIZABETH BARRETT

The world of literature is full of intimate love and romance stories of poets and writers in their personal life. Those who are familiar with English literature know the exciting love affairs of many renowned poets and writers of different countries. Nobody can forget the passionate love and marriage of Robert Browning (1812–1889) and Elizabeth Barrett (1806–1861). Both of them were exquisitely charming poets. Elizabeth was six years senior to Browning and was more popular and more established. They belonged to the Victorian era and appealed to the people with beautiful romantic poetry. Their love surpassed all physical boundaries and survived all objections and hostilities towards their love and led an exemplary life. They loved each other passionately and intimately cared and supported each other boundlessly. The profundity and ecstatic height of their love deeply fascinated the people then and continue to enchant the readers of their poetry even today albeit the lapse of almost two centuries.

Robert Browning and Elizabeth Barrett

Elizabeth Barrett Browning was the eldest of the twelve children of Edward Barrett and Mary Graham Clarke. She was a precocious child and even from childhood completely immersed in reading classic works. She studied Milton and Shakespeare during her teens. She published her first book of poetry at the age of twelve. But unfortunately she suffered from long illness and spinal injury from early teens. However despite ill health and financial downfalls of her father, she continued her creative writings.

Elizabeth became more and more melancholic and reclusive in daily life. She published a collection of poems in 1844 titled **Poems** and it drew the attention of famous English poet Robert Browning. He wrote to her in his first letter, "I love your verses with all my heart dear Miss Barrett". He praised her fresh, strange music, the affluent language, the exquisite pathos and true new brave thought. Earlier in 1842 when critics rejected Robert Browning's book **Dramatic Lyrics** Elizabeth had appreciated and defended the book and his innovative dramatic monologue style. They loved and appreciated each other's intellectual inclinations and poetic sensibilities.

Thus both of them started writing letters and through letters they exchanged their hearts also. They wrote each other as many as 600 beautiful love letters in about two years which are now esteemed as valuable legacy of the two great poets. Their passionate love culminated in their elopements and marriage in 1846. Barrett's father was violently against their marriage and opposed tooth and nail. He never changed his cruel and absurd attitude towards his daughter and did not talk to her again. He even refused to meet his grandson when they visited him with their son to mend the fence of relation. But he was adamant and uncompromising.

Robert Browning was born in 1812 as the only son of his parents. His father was a clerk in the Bank of England. He provided Robert with many books and this developed in him great interest in learning. By the age of fourteen he had achieved proficiency in English, French, Greek, Latin and Italian. He was a follower of Shelley's works. He profusely used the personal library of his father with 6000 volumes many of which were historical anecdotes which he used for his poetic creation. Although he joined the university college in London, he dropped out after the first year. His early period of literary career was dominated by his interest in dramas but later on he concentrated on poetry and introduced a new genre dramatic monologue. The Ring and the Book, (1868–69) a novel in verse and The Pied Piper of Hamelin a well known work in children's literature established him as a poet.

Browning's love and marriage with Elizabeth Barrett radically transformed the life of both. They went to Florence, Italy, the haven of poets and creative people and continued their poetic career. Elizabeth Barrett wrote beautiful love Sonnets dedicated to Browning. Her love sonnets are full of intense passion and emotional appeal. She wrote

"How do I love thee? Let me count the ways.
I love thee to the depth and breadth and height,
My soul can reach, when feeling out of sight,

....

I love thee with the breath,
Smiles, tears, of all my life; and if God choose,
I shall but love thee better after death." [Sonnet 43]

Browning-Barret love has no parallel in the world of English poetry. Both of them were equality brilliant and creative. They wrote poetry of profound love and passion, appreciated and evaluated each other's works. They had no professional jealousy and competition. It was a relationship like that of Jean Paul Sartre and Simon de Beauvoir, who remained lifelong friends in live-in relationship and shared their philosophical and literary ideas. They bore the criticism of the orthodox society but never relinquished their mutual companionship. Similarly Robert Browning and Elizabeth Barrett remained lifelong impeccable lovers and there was no scope for any alien feelings. They had only one powerful competition. Who will love deeper and more passionately? Browning wrote to Barrett,

"All my soul follow you – Love,
Encircled you and I live in being yours".

She wrote to him,

"I love you not only for what you are,
But for what I am when I am with you."

The incomparable feeling of inclusiveness and involvement makes love profoundly intimate. The unaffected feeling that I am also benefitted by your love is a magnificent thought that makes love reciprocal and spontaneous. The love of Barrett and Browning was genuine and a rare participation of one in the spiritual being of the other making the relation a marvellous communion.

A very enigmatic aspect of Barrett-Browning love is the incomprehensible power that united the two apparently incompatible persons. Robert Browning hailed from a prosperous family. He grew up in the happiest and the most stimulating atmosphere of the home. His father had a huge collection of books. He guided Robert with the help of those valuable books.

Elizabeth Barrett, on the other hand was a physically invalid girl brought up in a large family of twelve children. She was forced to confine herself to an isolated room. Her father was dominant and selfish. He was jealously fond of his daughter and did not even care to shift her to Italy for the sake of her health. He was blatantly against her love affair and marriage with Browning. In spite of many differences including age, the mysterious power of poetic spirit united them. It was not physical attraction or other external factors which united them. It was the divine attribute of love which united them. This exquisite union had made Barret physically comfortable in Florence.

Love despite illness, marriage despite objections survived because of their convictions and commitments. Barrett had tussled with the idea of surrendering to his love. She implored him not to get involved in love with an invalid who may relapse on precarious ground any time. She was not convinced of Browning love at first because of physical incapacity and age difference. But browning was an astute lover vigorous and extremely down to earth. It was in fact a marriage of minds and intellects.

All carnal calculations disappeared in such fabulous relationship. The poet lovers lived for each other. Browning instilled in her a new desire for life, and she on her part continued to be his source of inspiration. Barrett alone made any deep and abiding impression on his personality and poetic career. Browning wrote in his The Ring and the Book.

"Oh lyric love, half angel and half bird
And all a wonder, and a wild desire."

Love is the soul's way into a wider world. It is the exaltation of the finite towards the infinite. By love the personality can remain independent and yet not isolated. One personality mingles perfectly with another in an exquisite process of giving and gaining at the same time not losing its integrity. Thus love becomes a unique experience of man and is the basis of Brownian philosophy. Human love is the clearest manifestation of the infinite in the finites of the world. So love is a perpetual yearning of the soul to melt into the ultimate.

Browning and Barrett lived through this philosophy of love in their personal life. The ultimate revelation was the immaculate purity of their own love as manifested in the last years of their life in Italy. They in fact became soul-mates. Love gives the lover power to see the soul of the beloved and unite with the soul. True love is sublime and through it souls gain immortality. In his beautiful poem '**The Last Ride together**' Robert Browning expressed his own feelings and emotions to ride together to eternity.

"I and my mistress, side by side,
Shall be together breathe and ride,
So, one day more am I deified.
Who knows but the world may end to-night?

NINE

TWO EPIC LOVE STORIES

[I] PRITHVIRAJ CHOUHAN AND SANYOGITA

The epic love story of the 12th century legendary king Prithviraj Chouhan and the beautiful princess of Kannauj, Sanyogita is a fascinating saga of love, romance, war, and display of courage and chivalry. Prithviraj was a valiant Rajput king of India known far and wide for his exceptional bravery and intellectual acumen. His dynastic power and glory extended to a major part of north India. He had the credit of defeating the imperious Muslim invader Mohammed Ghori several times including the famous battle of Tarain in 1191. Prithviraj was well-versed in the art and science of warfare and had deep knowledge of a number of subjects including History, Mathematics, Philosophy, Theology, Painting and so on. Besides he was proficient in the art of archery, especially in blind folded condition following sound waves. He was a charismatic leader with extraordinary power and grit but unfortunately died at a very young age of 26 years.

The tales of Prithviraj Chouhan's reputation of valour and chivalry, and his splendid conquests reached the ears of Sanyogitha, the daughter of king Jaichand of Kannauj. Prithviraj was mesmerized by the captivating beauty of Sanyogitha. It was absolutely a reciprocal affair but was unacceptable to Jaichand. It is said that they fell in love when a painter exchanged their portraits. The relation between Jaichand and Prithviraj was strained due to their political ambitions and imperial aspirations.

Jaichand decided to organize Sanyogitha's 'Swayamvar' ceremony, the traditional Hindu custom of selecting bridegroom from among the assembled eligible royal bachelors. Jaichand deliberately did not invite Prithviraj with the obvious intention to insult him. To cause further humiliation Jaichand made a clay statue of Prithviraj and installed at the gate of the ceremonial hall as the doorkeeper. On the day of the ceremony Sanyogitha excluded the princes one by one with the bridal garland in her hands. Finally she garlanded the statue of her lover to the utter dismay of all those who were assembled there. Suddenly Prithviraj sprang from behind the statue and took Sanyogitha in his arms and whisked her away to Delhi.

The whole episode was executed with great speed and precision. The assembled princes and onlookers were taken aback at the unexpected turn of events. Prithviraj outsmarted Jaichand. Prithviraj was extremely infatuated with the beauty of his wife that he is said to have even neglected the state affairs. Jaichand, however, could not bear this insult and outrage on his authority. He forged an unholy alliance with Mohammed Ghori to avenge his humiliation. The Muslim interloper was waiting for such an opportunity. Prithviraj was defeated in the second battle of Tarain in 1192.

Sanyogitha eloping with Prithviraj from the "Swamwara"

The exhausted army of Prithviraj was surrounded by the enemies and his soldiers were engulfed in extreme panic and ran helter skelter. Prithviraj himself is said to have dismounted his elephant and fled from the battlefield on a horse. He was however captured and was made a vassal of the Ghori ruler. Nevertheless some time later Prithviraj rebelled against Mohammed Ghori. He refused to accept the hegemony of the sultan. Angry sultan got Prithviraj blinded with hot iron rods. Although blind Prithviraj shot arrow sensing air vibration and hit Ghori and killed him. Prithviraj's loyal court poet is said to have stabbed him and killed himself in order to escape further humiliation at the hands of the Ghori army.

It will be interesting to cite a fascinating parallel to the saga of Prithviraj and Sanyogitha from the medieval Scottish fables. The story of Lochinvar and his beloved Ellen evinces similarity of heroism and adventure in possessing the bride. The story is not corroborated by historical facts but has caught the imagination of the folk of Scotland. The nineteenth century Scottish poet Walter Scott (1771–1832) who imbibed extraordinary passion for the history of his country and love for its ballads and folklores immortalized the episode in his poem 'Lochinvar'. Scott transformed the folktale to a marvellous anecdote of love, romance, adventure and heroic chivalry of the protagonist.

Lochinvar was a young and brave knight of Scotland who was ardently in love with Princess Ellen. Lochinvar was a skilled fighter with tremendous confidence in his abilities to encounter the enemies. He was faithful in his love for Ellen and was equally fearless in war. He belonged to the class of charismatic knights who captured the imagination of beautiful damsels. Love for them meant romantic love mingled with chivalry and gallantry spirit. Lochinvar was endowed with all qualities which could captivate beautiful Ellen.

But destiny had some other design in store. Ellen's father vehemently opposed her marriage with Lochinvar. He clandestinely arranged her marriage with another man of his choice. The would-be groom was indeed "a laggard in love and a dastard in war". Ellen was bound to submit to the will of her parents. She was a damsel in distress unable to refrain from her love and forget her lover. She had no means to communicate with her lover about her dire dilemma.

However, Lochinvar had intimations about the happenings in the bride's family. He was aware of the inevitable plight of his beloved. He rushed to the wedding venue to rescue her. He was so valiant that no obstacle on the way could deter him from reaching his destination. He rode his robust horse almost unarmed and all alone. He did not stop on the way and swam across the river Eske. Lochinvar alighted at the gate of Netherby Hall where the ceremony was arranged. The hall was packed with people including bride's men and kinsmen, her brothers and relatives. The whole atmosphere was charged with surprises and apprehensions. The man who was about to make Ellen his bride was confused and utterly perturbed. He could not utter a word.

The bride's father stood up with his hand gripping his sword. He mustered courage and asked Lochinvar whether he had come in peace or with the intention of war or simply to dance at the bridal celebrations. Lochinvar boldly told that he loved his daughter passionately but he refused him the opportunity to marry her. He said, "Love swells like Solway but ebbs like its tide". He assured Ellen's father that he had abandoned his desire to possess her and he considered his love as love lost forever. He wanted only to dance and drink one cup of wine. Lochinvar declared in front of the tremulous crowd that there were more lovely maidens in Scotland who would gladly be ready to accept him as their groom.

He took the hand of Ellen and started dancing. She smiled and blushed. Their presence in the hall spread graceful radiance of love all around. The bride's maidens whispered that Lochinvar was best suited to Ellen. However the whole sequence of events infuriated the bride's father and fretted her mother. They could not do anything face-to-face with his elegant form and her lovely face. The hapless groom stood ashamed and unable to encounter the powerful rival.

Meanwhile Lochinvar whispered something in her ears near the door and with the lightning speed he mounted the horse with the lady in his arms and galloped away with her. For a while everything stood still. By the time people recovered from their momentary black out Lochinvar and Ellen were far from their vicinity. The clans tried to chase but of no avail. The bride was lost forever. Lochinvar proved to be, "daring in love and dauntless in war". The ballad of Lochinvar depicts the beautiful intricacies of love, romance, war and family relationships. Many factors interplay in the creative fulfilment of love. We see in the ballad the ultimate celebration of the victory of love.

Lochinvar and Ellen

(II) BAJIRAO AND MASTANI

LOVE BEYOND BARRIERS

There are love stories which surpass all socio-religious and geographical boundaries. One such story is that of the mighty Maratha Peshwa Bajirao and his bewitching paramour Mastani.

Their love and romance was one of the exciting and fabulous stories of Indian regal history. It crossed all boundaries of politics, religion, and conservative social norms. Their love surpassed all controls and stipulations of caste, creed and Brahmanic edict over even personal faith. Bajirao had to face the ire and fury of his family especially the distressing attitude of his first wife Kashibai. What infuriated the family of Bajirao and the conservative clan was that Mastani was a Muslim with mixed parentage. This in fact made their marriage a communion beyond all criteria and considerations of caste and community.

Bajirao and Mastani

The love and romance of Bajirao and Mastani amazes all even after 300 years. The fabulous story has been glorified in literature and of late in the beautiful movie directed by Sanjay Leela Bhansali in 2015. Historically Bajirao was elevated to the august office of Peshwa of Maratha Empire at the tender age of twenty. He fought more than 40 battles till his untimely death in 1740 at the age of only 39 years, emerging victorious in all battles.

Although he was a Brahmin by birth he was adept in the art of warfare and was instrumental in expanding Maratha Empire far and wide. He was a valiant fighter, smart strategist, intelligent and inspiring leader, and above all an extraordinary human being. The life of Bajirao was in fact a transformation from the duties of the caste to the duties of the state. The hands made for offering flowers to the deity preferred to hold the sword. The time meant for leisure and rest was devoted to make the enemies worried and restless. No wonder he was the greatest Maratha ruler after Shivaji Maharaj and the most popular and competent among all the Peshwas of the Marathas.

Shaniwar wada, Pune. The great seat of the Peshwas of the Maratha Empire

Bajirao's paramour the stunning and marvellous Mastani was the daughter of Maharaja Chhatrasal of Bundelkhand and his Muslim wife Ruhaani Bai Begum of Persian origin. Chhatrasal requested Bajirao's help to protect his state from the Muslim invader Muhammed Khan Bhangash. Bajirao defeated Bhangesh and restored the lost territory of Chhatrasal who out of gratitude and obligation offered his daughter Mastani in marriage to Bajirao already in love with her. Chhatrasal also granted the dominion over Jhansi, Saugar and Kalpi besides gold and precious gifts to Bajirao.

It must be remembered that Bajirao was already infatuated with the captivating beauty of Mastani. He agreed to the marriage proposal. The whole affair was the culmination of the events started with love at first sight. Mastani was a charming court dancer in her father's court and Bajirao fell in love with her during his very first meeting with Chhatrasal. The marriage however was not approved by Bajirao's orthodox family and the conservative society because of Mastani's Muslim heritage. Back in Pune Mastani lived for some time with Bajirao's famous place Shaniwarwada in the city. However because of the intolerance of the family towards Mastani, Bajirao built a separate residence for her at some distance from Shaniwarwada.

Mastani imbibed a liberal culture because of her cross breed background and also because her father Chhatrasal was a propagator of 'Pranami faith' that sought the unity of Islam and Hinduism. It is said that she was an ardent Krishna Bhakt and sang bhajans and offered Namaaz, kept vruta or fast according to Hindu custom and also followed Roza during Ramzan. A very commendable fact about her was that she was trained in martial arts, politics and diplomacy. She was very intelligent and was proficient in music and dance. She was endowed with extraordinary qualities of head, heart and hands.

Mastani bore a son who was initially named Krishnarao but custom bound conservative priests refused to conduct the Hindu 'Upnayana' ceremony because he was born to a semi-Muslim mother. They boy was eventually named Shamsher Bahadur and was brought up as a Muslim. After the death of Mastani in 1740, Bajirao's first wife Kashibai looked after the six year old Shamsher as her own son and bestowed upon him a portion of his father's dominion of Banda and Kalpi in the north.

There may have disputes and differences about the historical details and authenticity of the saga of Bajirao-Mastani, and their love, marriage and family life. But the whole episode is greatly appealing and captures our imagination. It was political expediency which prompted Bajirao to protect the interests of a Hindu king against a marauding Muslim invader. Bajirao accomplished that mission excellently with meticulous perfection. But what happened thereafter was inevitable. Two youngsters in the prime of youth experienced an emotional warfare and yearned for each other's heart. Bajirao defeated the enemy but was the victim of irresistible and alluring charm of Mastani. There was nothing unnatural about Bajirao's infatuation with Mastani because she was beautiful and talented. It is true that Bajirao was a married man and belonged to the orthodox Brahmin community. He held the high political office of the Peshwa and had the moral responsibility to uphold high moral standards and integrity in public life. But all the controls and inhibitions apart he was a man with all human frailties of the flesh.

The most laudable aspect of the love, romance and marriage was the courage displayed by Bajirao to marry a Muslim girl. He knew well the probable reactions and repercussions to his decision. The infallible fact that he was the Peshwa of the Maratha Empire might have stood in good stead against social ostracism. People didn't have the audacity to oppose the decision of the Peshwa. However Bajirao showed exceptional maturity of understanding amidst criticism and anger of the relatives. The love of Bajirao and Mastani was strong enough to face all adversaries and adversities. Love for them was their religion, their ultimate truth. Love that is fickle and weak to battle with the stormy sea is not love at all. Love is that power which can fight against the uncompromising world in front of everyone. There was no betrayal and cheating in the relationship of Bajirao and Mastani. That made it noble and exalted. They remained devoted to each other till death. They immortalized love through their exemplary life.

TEN

THREE ROMANTIC LOVE POETS

[1] BYRON [2] SHELLY [3] KEATS

(I) GEORGE GORDON BYRON

MAD, BAD AND DANGEROUS

The love story of George Gordon Byron, popularly known as Lord Byron (1788–1824) was one of the most adventurous and fascinating love stories of history. The history of English literature is full of enchanting stories and fables of love and romance. The sagas of his love and romance dominated romantic poetry. Byron's poetry obviously reflected the very emotional traits of his character. He possessed a personality, perhaps exclusively made for women. He was a rare and distinctive person who was positively besieged by women. The young women who met him fell flat for his love. Byron also responded quickly to any amorous advance. He started his love dalliance at the very tender age of eight years and continued till his death. The fabulous love stories and episodes of the love life of Lord Byron have captivated the minds of millions across the world.

George Noel Gordon, Lord Byron.

Lord Byron

Byron was the son of John Byron, a degenerate fellow with a nickname "Mad Jack", and Catherine Gordon, a rich and profligate heiress who was an alcoholic and of unstable mind. John Byron squandered her property and the family wealth gradually depleted. John Byron died when George Byron was only three years old. Byron had an unusual childhood because of the improper care of his governess and the unstable mental swings of his mother. He had a propensity to promiscuous relationship and homosexual tendencies from the very beginning. Although Byron had a deformity of the right foot he had a striking face and an impressive physical appearance.

No wonder his fellow poet Samuel Taylor Coleridge commented about his 'beautiful countenance'. He was a man of extremes in terms of mood and character. Walter Scott wrote of him, "his countenance was a thing to dream of. His glorious eyes, his mobile eloquent face fascinated all; he was, besides, a genius of the first rank". Byron described himself as "a strange mélange of good and evil".

Lord Byron had many lovers. Love was not an emotion to be sacrificed in one altar only. Love was Byron's most impelling emotion. He was made of soft and delicate love material. Byron wrote in a letter to Lady Melbourne in 1812 when he was 24 years of age, "I cannot exist without some object of love". Love was his very existence. He was a morbidly sensitive and sentimental boy and was remarkable for his emotional relationships. At the age of eight years he was in love with a girl named Mary Duft, and at ten he was in love with his cousin Margret Parker. And when he was fifteen he was enamoured by Mary Chaworth. She was two years his senior but refused to take the devotion of a school boy seriously. This unexpected refusal, however, caused great disappointment. He was distractedly in love with Chaworth. According to Caroline Byron "He was in love, in desperate love with her, which was worst of all tragedies". Byron himself wrote, "She was the beau ideal of all that my youthful fancy could point as beautiful". Byron found her celestial beauty and angelic nature as the ideal of love. His ideal of unattainable love was beyond sexuality.

Byron had a short but ardent love affair with Lady Caroline Lamb, married to William Lamb. The lady was fascinated by Byron's Childe Harold's' Pilgrimage. She described him as 'mad, bad and dangerous to know'. Byron was lack-lustre towards the lady's propensities and ended the relationship. Since she was obsessed with Byron she relapsed into desperation. She even entered his room dressed like a boy. She tried to stab herself and sent a snippet of hair to Byron in an envelope with a love letter signed "from your wild antelope". She was so obsessed that she burnt his effigy as in a pagan ritual to give vent to her frustration and nurtured a virulent hatred towards him for the rest of her life.

Byron was a prolific writer and equally prolific in love affairs. He was a celebrity with an impressive personality and dashing good looks and was the hot topic of every conversation. Men were jealous of him and women were jealous of each other. Byron had a long array of lovers both male and female in the short span of his life which lasted only for thirty six years. A few of the Byronic lady pyrogenic lovers were Mary Chaworth, Lady Caroline Lamb, Lady Melbourne, Anne Isabella Milbank, Augusta Leigh, Lady Jane Elizabeth Scott, Countess of Oxford, Teresa Contessa Guiccioli, The Macri Sisters (Katinkas, Mariana, Theresa, the maid of Athens), Elina da Mosta, Mariana, his lordships wife in Venice, Margarita Gonti, the bankers' wife etc. Besides these lady lovers there were gay lovers who influenced his personal and poetic life.

Byron had maintained a promiscuous relationship with his half sister Augusta Leigh. She was the daughter of his father's first wife Amelia. She married her cousin George Leigh, but the marriage turned to be an unhappy alliance. He gambled all his money and he left his wife and children nothing but tears and debts. Augusta had visited Byron while her husband and children were on a vacation. Byron's extreme relationship with Augusta led to her pregnancy and she delivered a baby girl in 1814 believed to be Byron's daughter.

While his relationship with Augusta continued Byron began to court Annabelle Milbank, a very intelligent and scholarly lady well-read in Mathematics, Philosophy and classical literature. She was a religious woman with strict morals. They met on many occasions and Byron was attracted by her modesty and intellect. Although she knew about Byron's weaknesses, still she fell wildly in love with him. She thought, although he is bad, he is very good at the same time. She considered it her duty to support him and improve his behaviour. They married in 1815, but made a huge mistake. The newly married couple visited Augusta when her husband was away. Annabelle slept alone in the Guest room while Byron and Augusta shared the master bed room.

That was the unfortunate beginning of their marital disaster. They separated after one year and

Annabelle left Byron with the child he had sired. They named the baby Ada Augusta. Annabelle in utter desperation revealed Byron's secrets to her parents, his incestuous relationships, abusive behaviour and uncontrolled anger. Everything became public secrets and Byron became a persona non grata in social circles. His reputation was damaged and was in utter financial crisis. He decided to leave England for good. He said, "England was unfit for me".

Byron left England in 1846 and went to Geneva with his English lover Claire Clairmont. There Claire became pregnant and gave birth to Byron's daughter Clara Allegra in 1817. He then discarded Claire and went to Italy and followed a string of loves in Italy. He wrote letters to his friends listing the women he had slept with in Italy including countesses, cobblers' wives and whores.

Byron's Italian lovers include Teresa Guiccioli who was married at the age of nineteen to a man more than forty years old. Teresa had met Byron just three or four days after her marriage with count Guiccioli and was fascinated by him. She was very beautiful with dreamy eyes and abundant golden hair. She was modest and graceful in behaviour. The Italian blonde and the English poet exchanged their hearts in no time. Byron responded to her thrilling passion with great fervour and intensity. She looked after him when he was ridden with fever. But her husband obviously disliked his wife's amorous audacity and took her away and even threatened Byron. Byron was in great despair, however exchanged many love letters.

Teresa had great admiration and adoration for Byron. Meanwhile he continued his remarkable literary activities. Teresa openly took up her abode with him till Byron left for Greece to aid them in their struggle for independence. Byron could not return to Italy and gave up his life in the battlefield. Byron's love for Teresa Guiccioli was genuine, a love which purified and exalted the dark and moody moments of Byron. Teresa left the pleasures of palace life and separated from her husband for the love of the poet lover.

Byron wrote to her "You sometimes tell me that I have been your first real love and I assure you that you shall be my first passion." When Byron boarded the ship to go to Greece to fight the war she broke down in tears as she said farewell to him. She spent twenty seven years after Byron's death in his memory as a widow. She published in 1886 her memoirs of the poet filled with interesting and affecting reflections.

There has been no parallel in literature to the insatiable love impetuosity of Byron. He wrote to his friends in 1810, "I am dying for the love of three Greek girls at Athens, three divinities", obviously referring to the Macri sisters,

"Maid off Athens, ere we part,
Give; oh give me back my heart"

Byron was the greatest of the romantic love poets for whom love was the source of inexorable creative energy. The variety, immensity, and intensity and perhaps indiscreet love enriched literature with exquisitely beautiful love poetry.

<<<<<>>>>>

(II) PERCY BYSSCHE SHELLEY (1792–1822)

THE INTELLECTUAL LOVER

All those who love Shelley, the 'mad Shelley', love him for his bold ideals, unconventional moral sense, beautiful lyric poetic creations and above all the magnificent humanism. Nobody can forget the melancholy tinged lines, "I fall upon the thorns of life! I bleed!" All appreciate even the pessimism of "we look before and after, and pine for what is naught" and the optimism of the famous lines "Oh wind, if winter comes can spring before behind?" Poet-philosopher Shelley was one of our most familiar young romantic poets who established a marvellous position in English literature through his beautiful romantic poems. He was young and ebullient, emotionally sensitive and strong in his convictions. There was a note of sadness in his poetry as in his personal love life. Unfortunately he died at the prime of his youth.

Shelley's first love was Harriet Westbrook, daughter of a successful coffee house owner. He met her at London in 1811. She was intelligent and charming, and wrote passionate love letters to Shelley. She was impressed by Shelley's poetic genius and revolutionary ideals. Shelley also reciprocated with love and soon their intimacy became inseparable. Harriet even threatened to end her life because of her unhappiness at home and in the school. They eloped to Scotland to get married. Shelley was nineteen and Harriet just sixteen, and were at the peak of adolescent infatuation.

However both their families expressed surprise at the unexpected decision of the youngsters. Harriet involved herself whole heartedly in Shelley's literary and socio-political activities. Harriet's elder sister Eliza came to stay with them shortly after their elopement. Her stay was instrumental in many frictions in their family life. They remarried in 1814 in a London church in order to provide legal protection to their daughter. Meanwhile Shelley developed an extramarital affair with Mary Godwin, a novelist and the daughter of William Godwin. This obviously led to the emotional separation of Shelley and Harriet. Harriet was extremely dejected because she was already in her advanced stage of pregnancy. In 1816 because of uncontrollable depression she drowned herself in the river near Hyde Park. She was hardly twenty one years old when she died leaving behind her daughter and the husband who deserted her.

Shelley

One of the reasons for Harriet's exit from Shelley's life and from the world itself was the illicit entry of his second love Mary Godwin. She was perhaps more compatible to Shelley emotionally and intellectually. Shelley wanted his soul-mate to feel his poetry and understand his philosophy. Mary Godwin born in 1797 at London was the daughter of William Godwin a philosopher and political writer, and Mary Wollstonecraft who died shortly after her birth. The situation in the family changed when Godwin married Clairmont, mother of two children. Godwin used to have many distinguished visitors including great poets like William Wordsworth and Samuel Taylor Coleridge.

Shelley was a devoted student of Godwin and used to visit their house frequently. He was fascinated by Mary and forgot the reality that he was a husband and a father. Mary who was under the torturous stepmother felt attraction for the young scholar. She found an outlet for her pent up emotions. Shelley and Mary eloped accompanied by Mary's step sister, Jane. Mary wrote to Shelley in 1814, "We will defy our enemies and our friends (I see they are all as bad as one another) and will not part again". Mary's action alienated her from her father who did not speak to her for a long time. They travelled from place to place and faced many difficulties. They married legally in 1816 and in 1818 Mary wrote the famous monster tale of Frankenstein or the modern Prometheus. The book was a great success. However the greatest tragedy occurred in 1822. Shelley drowned in the gulf of Spezia when the boat he was travelling capsized.

Shelley presented a cosmic idea of love and devoted his life to the pursuit of perfect love. The story of his life was an incessant search for such love in different hues as sexual love, platonic love, cosmic love and love of humanity. Love is the governing principle of nature. All things are forever trying to unite with the spirit of divine love.

"Nothing in the world is single;
All things by law divine;
In One spirit meet and mingle,
Why not I with thine?"

The same spirit is expressed in the lines in the elegy **Adonais** "The One remains; the many change and pass..." Love is free and is the greatest source of benefits to the lover and the beloved. They encourage each other for the practice of virtues and noble things. Shelley's philosophy was nobler and higher than sexual feelings and carnal pleasures. However love seems to exclude commitment and hence the institution of marriage has no relevance. To promise love for the same woman for ever is absurd. He himself deserted Harriet and pursued the love of Mary Godwin. Husband and wife must live united if at all they love each other. Even a law which binds them to cohabit without love is simply an intolerable imperiousness and a burden beyond toleration. Love is the basic philosophy of life. He wrote,

"What is all this sweet work worth?
If thou kiss not me?"

(III) JOHN KEATS AND FANNY BRAWNE

LOVE WITHOUT FANFARE

John Keats (1795–1821) was a prominent poet among the younger generation of romantic poets. He was the eldest of the four surviving children of Thomas Keats and Frances Jennings. The children became orphans at their early age and their maternal grandparents looked after them. Keats had an insignificant infatuation with Isabella Jones, a beautiful, talented and well-read girl, whom he befriended in early 1817. Keats did not hesitate to accept his sexual attraction and feeling of warmth in her proximity. However Keats meeting with Fanny Brawne at the end of 1818 transformed the whole episode of life. Fanny was Keats' neighbour at Hampstead where she was staying with her widowed mother and two siblings. Keats was in the midst of great personal turmoil. His youngest brother Tom was desperately ill with tuberculosis. It had already taken the life of his mother and Keats was also in the grip of the malady.

Keats

Fanny Brown was eighteen years old and although not very beautiful, was very spirited and kind. She was a realist and was very practical perhaps due to the peculiar circumstance in the family. She was highly impressed by the interesting conversation of Keats when they met. Keats visited her frequently and each time the brown haired, blue-eyed Fanny made great lasting impression on him. Now all his desires were concentrated on Fanny. It was during those two or three years that Keats wrote most of his best creations including the great Odes. Fanny 'confused and exasperated' Keats, and that was the magic of her attraction. Keats wrote about her to his bother as a beautiful, silly, fashionable and strange girl. Meanwhile poetry had become Keats primary passion. Keats romance blossomed and he started writing sonnets to Fanny. Most of these works dwell upon external beauty and physical charm and the pleasant sensation of sensuousness.

Thus the first powerful love affair gave him new impetus, new inspiration and new insight into his own emotions. His poetry began to reflect power of personal perception and maturity of emotions. He once wrote to Fanny, "I have two luxuries to brood over in my walks, your loveliness and the hour of my death."

He wrote Again,

"My love has made me selfish,
I am forgetful of everything,
But seeing you again."

Keats composed the best loved works, "La Belle Dame Sans Merci," "Ode to Grecian Urn", "Ode to Nightingale," "Ode to Melancholy' fallowed by Lamia, Isabella, The Eve of St. Agnes and other poems in 1820.

However as summer waned the condition of his lungs deteriorated. Doctors warned that his lungs would not survive another winter in England. So Keats went to Italy with his friend painter Joseph Severn.

The excruciating moment came when he had to say farewell to Fanny Brawne. But that was inevitable. Both said farewell to each other knowing very well that a happy return was impossible. Keats died of tuberculosis, his 'family disease' on 23 February 1821 in Rome at the tender age of twenty five. It was after his death that his reputation had grown far beyond anything he experienced in his life time. He had once rightly said, **"I think I shall be among the English poets after my death."**

Keats beloved fiancée Fanny was deeply pained by the death of her lover. They were supposed to marry after his return from Italy. But they were not destined to live as soul mates. Fanny Brawne led a life of mourning for many years and in 1833 she married Louis Lindo and they had three children. In 1865 before her death Fanny told her children about the love letters of Keats, "the relics of that romance". Herbert and Margret Lindo got all the love letters published after the death of their father in 1872.

The love and romance of Keats and Fanny Browne was most exciting and extraordinary. It was an intimacy of two or three years but was an immortal love relation. Keats wrote in one of his letters "My love is selfish. I cannot breathe without you". There was some kind of excruciating factors in their love; it was a kind of madness. However their love was not superficial and peripheral; it was profound and penetrating; it was a soul to soul, heart to heart relation. We find in their love all permeating elements of truth and goodness. He said, 'Truth is beauty and beauty is truth". Love mingles with truth and beauty. They realized truth and beauty in their love. As a result of this vision they could love each other despite the fatal disease which was killing him slowly.

To love and to be loved are not very great things; whereas to love someone who is ailing is a divine form of love. For Keats Fanny Brawne was the 'Bright Star'. It was indeed the glittering star called Fanny Brawne which illumined the life of Keats, and inspired his creative poetic genius.

ELEVEN

LAYLA AND MAJNUN

THE TRAGEDY OF MAD LOVE.

"A fire burnt within his heart,
All through the days and nights dark".

Nizami Ganjavi [1141–1209 A.D]

Romantic love is the splendour of transforming everything into fascinating experiences. Even the ugliest things appear as the most beautiful ones. The detestable objects look lovable and attractive. The exquisite bond of love of two persons causes a sudden metamorphosis. Sometimes the change is tragic and sometimes unexpected. The strings of love are capable of producing exquisite mellifluous melody if they are properly fixed and tightened. On the contrary if the strings are broken or kept loose they cannot produce melodious music. The lost love like the broken string is unable to create a harmonious strain.

The stories of romantic love dalliance will be incomplete without refreshing the most captivating love story of the east – **'Layla and Majnun**' immortalized by the ebullient Persian poetic genius Nizami Ganjavi. Every nation has its fabulous tales of love to emulate; every culture has a few romantic tales as their emotional heritage; every literature is replete with a wealth of tales of love and romance. They form their rich and abundant cultural and literary reservoirs. Europe in the past had their marvellous Abelard and Heloise, Petrarch and Laura, Dante and Beatrice, while Arabia can be proud of its unparalleled Layla and Majnun.

The legend of Layla and Majnun has an amazing Arabic origin. The story with all its fascinating elements of history and imagination, myth and truth, love and lunacy, and the quest for communion spread to the other parts of the world through Persian, Turkish and Indian languages. The story became the most popular love theme in the writings of great poets. One of the most powerful emulations of love can be found in famous Persian poet Nizami's popular narrative poem **Layla-Majnun**. Lord Byron described the poem as "the Romeo and Juliet of the East", although it was composed almost four hundred years before Romeo and Juliet.

The magnificent love story is based on the real heart rending love story of a young man named Qays ibn al-Mullawah (645–688 AD) an Arabic poet of the seventh century. He fell madly in love with Layla al -Aamiriya, a not so beautiful girl born in a rich and aristocratic family who lived a life of splendour and plenty. They loved each other and were consumed in intense passion and panting for each other. Love conquered them and they never dreamt to part. Qays composed splendid romantic poems and dedicated them to his lady love mentioning her name frequently in the poem. Qay's friends made fun of his love for Layla as crazy madness. But Qays was unmoved and unruffled, and was unmindful of the taunts and scorns of his friends. His eccentricities were inseparable from his very existence.

"No rest he found by day or night,
Layla for ever in his sight"

Qays was a great poetic genius but was financially poor far below Layla's rich family. He however decided to ask Layla in marriage from her parents. But Layla's father promptly refused an alliance with a man of low social status which would be a scandal according to the Arab traditions.

Now the vigilant father sequestered his daughter and ensured that she did not have any contact with her crazy lover. However, as in Nizami narration of Layla and Majnun she said to her father,

"If meeting of lovers is a sin,
I shall not go to school again
And live in your sweet company"

Layla's parents married her off to a wealthy man. This was intolerable to Qays and he was totally heart-broken.

Qays alienated himself from the tribe and wandered in the surrounding desert with a broken heart. The abjectly desperate family made frantic efforts to ensure his normal life but all in vain. Eventually they gave up all hope. Qays lived in isolation composing poems for his beloved in utter despair and dejection. He could be seen ranting poetry to himself and inscribing Layla's name in the sand with a stick. He was overpowered by the thoughts of his lost beloved day in and day out. It was a kind of possession due to obsession in love.

Qays' parents shattered by the sorrow of their missing son breathed their last after years of futile waiting. Layla was determined to inform Majnun the sad news of their demise. She begged an old man who claimed to have seen Majnun during his travels. One day the old man delivered the painful news to Majnun. It was a terrible blow to the poet already at the depth of despair. Thereafter unable to overcome the sorrow he alienated himself entirely from the ruthless world and vowed to live in the desert and wilderness amidst wild animals as his companions.

Layla too was in a devastating mental condition. She was shattered in mind, body and spirit. The distressed damsel could not bear the life thrust upon her by her parents. After the death of her husband she wanted to be with her first love. But ironically the tradition demanded that she must remain in her home alone for two years without seeing another human being. This was unbearable for her who had already lived a life of separation from her love. Finally she fell ill and died. Qays' friends wanted to inform him about the tragic end of Layla but they could not trace him. Not much later however Qays was found dead in the wildness near an unknown woman's grave!

Qays went mad for his love. He was crazy and for this reason he was called Majnun-Layla which means 'driven mad by Layla'. He wrote the following touching lines which depicted his mental condition.

"I pass by these walls, the walls of Layla,
And kiss this wall and that wall,
It is not love of the walls,
That has enraptured my heart,
But of the one who dwells within them."

Long before Nizami the poet who immortalized the story of Layla and Majnun the legend of the lovers had spread in the form of anecdotes in many parts of the Persian countries. The anecdotes were mostly transmitted orally and were loosely joined without compact connections. It was Nizami who collected the secular and mystical elements of the story and portrayed a lively picture of the ardent lovers with necessary poetic embellishments and modifications of the plot. Subsequently many Persian poets imitated Nizami and wrote their own versions of the romance. The poem depicted the various aspects of love and romance characterized by the attraction for the beloved and the non-fulfilment of the aspirations of the lovers.

Interestingly the number and range of anecdotes about lovers increased considerably from the twelfth century. The mystical writers contrived many different stories about 'Majnun' to illustrate the mystical aspects of love-madness. These writers, known as the Sufi writers, used the name Layla to refer to the very concept of love. In Arabic language Layla means 'night', obviously referring to the fact that the romance of the lovers was hidden and kept as a secret. Majnun alludes to the one who is completely possessed or a person madly in love, a maniac, a lunatic or a crazy person.

According to one popular belief the graves of Layla and Majnun are situated in a village in an Indian state Rajasthan. The legend depicts that Layla-Qays hailed from Sindh province and came to the village to escape the fury of Layla's parents and her brother who blatantly opposed the love and romance of Layla and Majnun. The eloping lovers however could not cross the desert because of a terrible sand dune and ultimately surrendered to ruthless hunger and thirst in the desert. The lovers embraced death in the desolate wilderness of the remote village. Thus the village became a symbol of unconsummated love. Their beautiful mausoleum is believed to have become a centre of pilgrimage for lovers, would-be lovers and newly- weds from far and wide.

The legend has yet another dramatic variation according to which Layla and Majnun were enamoured as students. The headmaster used to beat Majnun for his juvenile infatuation for Layla and thereby neglecting his studies. But Majnun had only one thought in his mind. All other thoughts disappeared when the thought of the beloved occupied the mind of the lover. He told to the teachers and friends about this love, "It is a hunger of hearts in love, not simply an amorous deed. But strangely whenever Majnun was beaten Layla would bleed.

The families were exasperated and were unable to control the crazy behaviour of Majnun. They decided to prevent Layla and Majnun from seeing each other. However, they met again in their youth and Majnun wanted to marry Layla. The infuriated brother of Layla challenged Majnun and in a quarrel Layla's brother was killed. Majnun was arrested and was sentenced to be stoned to death. Layla could not bear the agony and agreed to comply with the wish of the family to marry another man provided Majnun was exempted from capital punishment and instead be awarded a minor punishment such as exile from his village. Thus Layla was married to another man of her parents' choice and Majnun was exiled. He was destined "to live a life of loneliness and dream of a denied love".

Layla's heart however yearned for Majnun and her angry husband challenged Majnun to death. Layla's husband's sword pierced the heart of Majnun and instantly Layla collapsed at her home and died. They were buried in adjacent graves and their souls met in heaven to lead an everlasting life together free from the cruelties and iniquities of the unkind society. They became immortal.

The credit of collecting, reviving and replenishing the traditional legends and anecdotes in the form of a beautiful narrative poem goes to poet Nizami Ganjavi, five hundred years after the death of Qays and Layla. Hundreds of versions of Qays-Layla love and romance episodes have been published, in many languages across the world. Nizami's masterpiece Layla-Majnun has been translated into many languages from the original Persian. The great work was translated into

English by James Atkinson in 1835. This fascinating love story has been rendered into novels, dramas, ballets, musical compositions, besides innumerable films in different languages. Layla and Majnun are glorified creations symbolizing love, lunacy, mysticism and perpetual yearning for communion.

It will be useful to know about the celebrated poet of Layla-Majnun, who revolutionized the genre of love poetry. He was Nizami Ganjavi, a twelfth century Persian poet adorable as the greatest romantic poet of Persian literature. Nizami was not a court poet and therefore did not figure in the record of dynastic rulers. He was born in the year 1141 in the city of Ganja in Azerbaijan with predominantly Iranian population. He died in the year 1209 at the age of sixty eight. His father was Yusuf as mentioned once in his poetry, and mother was Raisa with Kurdish background. His personal name was Ilyas and Nizami was his pen-name. Nizami was orphaned at a very young age and was raised by his maternal uncle Kwaja Umar who gave him excellent education.

Nizami married three times. His first wife was named Kipchak a slave girl sent to him by the ruler of Darband as a gift. She was Nizami's 'most beloved' wife and had a son by her. Nizami's two other wives also had premature death, incidentally coinciding with the completion of an epic. This prompted him to bewail, "O God why is it that for every 'Mathnavi' I must sacrifice a wife?"

Although Nizami was not a philosopher in the strict sense as Avicenna (980–1037 AD) was, he inculcated deep philosophic thoughts in his poetry.

He was a learned poet and a master of mellifluous and sensuous poetic style. Nizami was well-versed in Arabic and Persian literatures. He was an incomparable scholar with deep knowledge of subjects ranging from Mathematics to Ethics, Medicine to Mythology, Geology to Geography, Astrology to Asceticism, and Theology to the Theory of Law. He was a renowned scholar of Islamic studies and Koranic exegesis.

Nizami was an ardent follower of Firdausi (940-1020 AD) the celebrated Persian poet, and the author of the marvellous work **Shahnama (Book of King**s). Nizami read this masterpiece work several times with profound interest. Nizami used Shahnama as the source of his three epics-**Haft Peykar** (Seven Beauties), **Khosrous and Shirin**, and the third **Eskandar Namesh** (The Book of Alexander).

Nizami used the Arabic anecdote of Qays and Layla and infused in it a strong and captivating Persian flavour. An important aspect of Layla and Majnun is the humanistic approach of the poet towards lovers. There is a deep lying Sufi strain of superior love in Layla-Majnun. Hafiz (1315–1390) a well known Persian poet of love and wine who opposed religious hypocrisy and pretensions remarked about Nizami.

"Not all treasured store of ancient days,
Can boast the sweetness of Nizami's lays."

There is no convincing parallel to Nizami's Layla-Majnun in the world of literature of love poetry. The two lovers live in the world of different and strange dimensions. Layla's love is quiet and she is unable to express her love boldly in front of her parents. She is bound by circumstances.

"Like a bird imprisoned in a cage,
Layla bemoaned all day and night,
Longing for the idol unique."

(Layla-Majnun: Canto V)

Poetry is the passionate language of a devoted lover. The passion of Majnun is uncontrollable and he declares his obsession publicly in sorrowful lyrics for all to hear. He is not afraid of ranting passionate verses about the beauty of Layla. The voice reached Layla because even the children and every passer-by were humming his love songs. Layla quietly bore the agony.

"She lived between the water of her tears,
And the fire of her love....."

Majnun was overcome with painful sense of sorrow, grief and rejection. He abandoned everything and moaned in the solitude of wilderness. He befriended wild animals and continued to write and recite poetry of passion and obsession about his love for Layla. Majnun lived the life of a solitary ascetic hermit. However his soul was perpetually bonded to Layla. They were spiritually and emotionally inseparable. Lovers can be physically separated but cannot be mentally alienated. A fire burnt within his heart day and night.

There was no cure for love-sick Majnun. No one has ever cured a patient of love. Parents, friends, relatives, well-wishers and pious counsellors tried to efface Layla from Majnun's mind. Even the king felt compassion for the crazy young man. He told the anguished Majnun that Layla was not a beautiful woman and if at all she was very fascinating she would have been in the King's harem. The king even offered Majnun the most beautiful woman of his harem. Majnun looked at each woman and said while passing, "This is not my Layla"! Someone suggested that they would bring a thousand charming maidens fairer than Layla. But Majnun replied, 'O! To see the beauty of Layla the eyes of Majnun are needed'. A very touching aspect of their love is depicted in these lines,

"His love's lunacy grew more and more,
At last giving up all his hopes,
He sank in drowning deep despair."

The parents were hopeful of saving their son from the depth of desperation through divine intercession. As the last resort they made effort to rescue their son from the clutches of infatuation. Majnun's hapless father took him to Holy Kaaba, the ultimate place of pilgrimage. He hoped to cure his son of his obsession with Layla who had already married another man. However, the beleaguered lover prayed to Allah the most beneficent and merciful, more ardently and distressingly to make his love stronger and more sincere in his devotion and commitment.

Majnun was convinced that his love for Layla transcended all physical contacts, sensuality, lust and selfish interests. True love demanded sacrifice, and the perpetual quest for fulfilment. Layla was the symbol of divine beauty and the paragon of perfect love: the love that never questions, the love that never challenges the lover. Majnun experienced purification of his soul from the darkness of lust, low desires, and the feeling of shame.

He reached the Sufi state of 'Fana' or annihilation of the self and the communion with the ultimate truth the Beloved. Love has exalted him to the state of mysticism where he was liberated from the extremes of the flesh. He lived in the spirit of Sufi saints – minimum food, minimum speech and minimum sleep. His love was hunger for the ultimate, the quest to be one with the ultimate God. "All hungers die into one hunger Supreme".

The course of true love never did run smooth,

Lovers and madmen have such seething brains,

Such shaping fantasies that apprehend,

More than cool reason ever comprehends,

The lunatic, the lover, and the poet,

Are of imagination all compact.

{Shakespeare: A Midsummer Night's Dream}

xxxxxxxxxxxx

TWELVE

PRINCE SALIM AND ANARKALI

The love affair of the Mughal prince Salim and the humble courtesan Anarkali is one of the most popular and touching love stories of the past. It has become more popular and appealing after the release of the famous movie Mughal-e-Azam in 1960 with its punch dialogues and mesmerizing lyrics. The captivating lines "Pyar kiya to darna kya", "Pyar kiya koi chori nahi kiya" etc are like revolutionary slogans for lovers. This spectacular love legend has almost radically transformed the notion of romantic love among the younger generation.

Historical facts and events apart the marvellous love story evinces extraordinary power of fascination. It has an inherent power to captivate our imagination. There are disputes and differences of opinion among historians and chroniclers regarding the historical authenticity of the existence of Anarkali. However there is no dearth of information regarding the history of Salim who later on became the infamous emperor of Mughal Empire. It is futile to investigate pure historical facts in a love story, because a love story is infused with creative imagination.

The love legend of Salim and Anarkali is a real life story. It contains history mingled with romance, passion, melodrama, and emotional climax. There is anger, defiance, violence, tragedy and ultimate discomfiture in it. It is one of the deeply sentimentalized and widely sensationalized love stories of the world because of its tragic finale. This epic love legend transcends time and space and emerges in our mind as one of the best emotion filled love stories.

According to history Prince Salim, later with the regal name Jahangir, was the son of Mughal Emperor Akbar born to one of his wives in 1569 A.D. Anarkali with her childhood name Sharifun-Nissa, also known as Nadira Begum, hailed from Persia and was a courtesan in the Mughal court at Lahore. She was called Anarkali meaning "Pomegranate blossom" an epithet purported to have been given by Akbar fascinated by her bewitching beauty and physical attraction. She was a marvellous dancer and singer and used to perform as a courtesan in royal gatherings. She could enthral the audience with her magnificent performance.

Although Anarkali came from an ordinary slave family she had all those qualities which could enamour any young man. Prince Salim saw Anarkali during a dance performance and instantly fell in love with her. Although it is forbidden for a prince to love someone below the rank, Salim crossed all the boundaries and defiantly started courting the courtesan. Gradually Anarkali also started experiencing a romantic crush and reciprocated the love of the prince. Soon an intense and inseparable relation developed between them. They met frequently and shared their joys and sorrows intimately. They were so passionate in love that a separation was impossible and inconceivable for the lovers.

The clandestine romance of the prince and the low-born courtesan soon became public and obviously reached the ears of Akbar. Akbar was infuriated by the prince's alliance with an ordinary courtesan of low birth and outright rejected the relationship. After a violent altercation and argument between the angry father and the defiant son, an enraged Akbar ordered his guards to arrest and put Anarkali in prison.

However it is said that Salim with the help of his close friends helped Anarkali to escape to the outskirts of Lahore. Meanwhile Salim formed an army of his own and revolted against his father in vain. The mighty army of Akbar easily defeated the slender force of Salim. Akbar warned his vanquished son either to surrender Anarkali or be ready for death penalty. His deep love for Anarkali did not allow him to betray her and instead accepted death penalty.

When Anarkali came to know about the fate of her lover she rushed to the Emperor and pleaded to spare Salim's life. As expected the emperor agreed and as per her last wish Anarkali prayed to the king to allow her to spend one night with her beloved which the emperor readily granted. Anarkali is said to have applied pomegranate blossom to make the prince unconscious so as to avoid any confrontation with the guards. The next morning the guards came and dragged Anarkali amidst heart-wrenching scenes of agony and tears. According to the legend she was entombed in a brick wall, the most brutal and inhuman way of giving capital punishment.

However according to another legend Akbar spared the life of Anarkali on a promise that she would never ever see Salim again and allowed her to escape. It is said the brick wall was connected to a secret tunnel through which Anarkali escaped to some unknown destination. This version may be a ploy to present the emperor as a kind and compassionate man who respected humanity and the dignity of woman.

The exact historical time line of the events of Anarkali's life especially after the royal punishment is not very clear. However it is believed that after her supposed escape from punishment Anarkali went to Lahore where she lived until her death in 1599 A.D. She was buried there and in 1615 the love sick Prince, already Emperor Jahangir, built a tomb for his beloved. There is a gravestone with a touching inscription in Persian which means-

"Ah! Could I behold the face of my beloved once more,

I would remain thankful to Allah till the day of resurrection".

Below this inscription the name of the composer is written as "Majnun Salim Akbar" meaning "Enamoured Salim, son of Akbar". This is the only indication that Anarkali is buried in the tomb and for centuries the local people of Lahore have believed that a beautiful dancer named Anarkali is buried there. Historians however differ in their views on the identity of the tomb. Some say that the so-called tomb of Anarkali actually is of a lady named Sahib-e-Jamal, another wife of Salim and the mother of his second son Sultan Parvez.

The fabulous love story of Salim and Anarkali has a very different version transmitted from one generation to another through oral and written means. A British traveller and trader during 1608 to 1611 A.D., William Finch mentions that Anarkali was one of the wives of Akbar and the mother of Daniyal. Akbar was suspicious about her incestuous liaison with his son Prince Salim for which she was entombed alive. Edward Terry who visited a few years after Finch wrote that Akbar threatened to disinherit Jahangir for his illicit liaison with Anarkali, the Emperor's most beloved wife. Another writer Noor Ahmed Chishti wrote in 1860 A.D. that Anarkali was a very beautiful lady and the favourite concubine of Akbar. Akbar's over-indulgent love for Anarkali made his other wives jealous and hostile to Anarkali.

The whole romantic legend of Salim and Anarkali is filled with history, mystery, fury, jealousy and conspiracy. The life of Anarkali is more mysterious and fascinating than the life of Salim. Anarkali was a very talented and stunningly beautiful courtesan and a marvellous dancer and singer in the court of Akbar. Obviously lascivious and lewd as he was Akbar might have forced her to be his concubine. It is unlikely that Anarkali had any emotional attachment to the father-like figure. Hence Anarkali's love for the young and ebullient prince Salim was natural. The whole episode seems to be entangled in a love triangle in which the son is the hero and the father a stubborn villain.

Whatever may be the historical intricacies of the Salim-Anarkali love story its popularity and appeal is on account of the heart-rending tragedy that had befallen on poor Anarkali. Prince Salim was the son of a mighty emperor and had all the resources at his disposal. However there existed an inexplicable bond of love between the noble prince and the low-born courtesan. Akbar tried to dissuade the lovers by using all sorts of tactics to denigrate the girl in front of the love-smitten son. The innocent Anarkali was unaware of the imminent threat hidden in her infatuation. She had to pay heavily for her audacity to love a prince who proved to be incapable of defending and protecting her life from the barbaric decision of his father.

It is baffling that a licentious and voluptuous emperor as Akbar with three dozen wives and hundreds of women in the harems should oppose his son's love for Anarkali.

Anarkali warrants our sympathy and compassion because of her suffering and sacrifice for the sake of her love for the prince. Prince Salim although depicted as a passionate lover who laments over his lost love was not ready to sacrifice his life for his beloved. No doubt he reacted defiantly and even revolted against his father allegedly for the sake of Anarkali. However the real cause of the revolt was in fact was his impatience to ascend to the throne.

The crown prince had to wait till the age of 36 years to succeed to the Mughal throne putting an end to fifty years of his father's long regime. An ambitious son like Salim wanted power in his hands at the earliest possible opportunity. Mughal history is full of royal intrigues, conspiracies and homicides in order to capture power and then to remain in power. Love is only a palpable means to fulfil salacious behaviour and satisfy carnal pleasures.

The legend of Salim-Anarkali is painful because of its underlying melancholy and pathos. The story is intimately personal and rends our hearts at the very thought of the savage way in which she was interred in the wall. Imagine the defenceless girl panting for breath in her claustrophobic enclosure and bearing the pangs of death inch by inch. Readers, listeners and viewers of this pathetic and distressing story cannot restrain tears because it is an extremely woeful tale of an ill-fated girl. Her only mistake was that she reciprocated the love of the Prince. If she had refused to respond to his love she would have been forcibly thrown into the harem or brutally killed for which the Mughal emperors were notorious.

Prince Salim has often been projected and glorified as a paragon of pure romantic love. However his very attitude and responsibility in the whole episode of love is incomprehensible and does not fit in the spirit of a real passionate lover. He could not satisfactorily justify and defend his love in front of his father. He was not ready to renounce the comforts and pleasures of the palace. Even Akbar's anger towards Salim and the alleged punishment for defiance and revolt appear ploys to give the impression that the emperor was just and impartial. Salim must have strongly stood by his love and must have shown readiness to sacrifice his life and embrace death with joy. He had displayed great courage and determination in his love which is reflected in these challenging words-

"Today I will narrate the true story of my heart,
Even if the world takes away my life."

The courage and confidence of the Prince seems to have drained away face-to-face with the imperious emperor.

There is another reason to suspect the sincerity of Salim in his love for Anarkali. He was a Prince surrounded by countless wives, concubines, consorts, courtesans and bewitching beauties all around. He was a alcohol addict and was a salacious king with more than 300 beautiful women in his harem to share his bed besides 26 wives whom he acquired from different regions of the Mughal empire by force or through political negotiations. How can such a polygamous philanderer be honestly faithful to one woman, that too, a courtesan of poor and humble birth?

"Man loves only once in this world with someone,
Then he lives with that pain and dies with that pain."

These words are spontaneous overflow of powerful feelings of love-smitten Prince Salim in a state of despair as depicted in films and fictions. He was stating a universal truth about lost romantic love towards one lover. However where there are multiple love affairs as in the case of the Mughal despots love simply means erotic fulfilment. The actual mental condition of Salim after the execution of Anarkali cannot be ascertained for sure because he had not mentioned anything about his lost love in his memoirs **Tuzk-i-Jahangiri** written in Persian. May be that he wanted to avoid the stigma about his amorous appetite towards a courtesan of low birth and inferior position. By all standards however the pathetic love legend of Prince Salim and Anarkali is a marvellous historic episode immortalized through the imagination of creative writers.

THIREEN

GIACOMO CASANOVA

THE INFAMOUS PHILANDERER AND WOMANIZER

Everyone in the world is familiar with the eighteenth century magic name Casanova [1725–1798] a man known for seducing women and having many lovers. Women were terribly charmed by his captivating personality. Casanova is now the symbol of love, romance, passion and serial seductions. Casanova, the incorrigible Venetian lover is an appellation for an unscrupulous womanizer and a philanderer. He is a synonym for a person who indulges in exorbitant sexuality and sensual indulgences. Casanova possessed all those qualities of a man which spontaneously attracted women of all ages and positions.

Casanova was in fact a weakness of women. His mesmerizing nearness ensnared them. The legendary lover proceeded passionately from one romantic conquest to another. The story of this prolific philanderer who gained the dubious reputation as a sex adventurer from Venice is extremely interesting and exciting. Casanova described his personal experiences in his famous autobiography **The History of My Life**, a monumental work of more than 4000 pages in 12 volumes which was published posthumously. It is the original source of information about this extraordinary man and his exotic life of pleasure hunting. His fabulous memoirs reveal his clandestine relation with women who loved him because of his peculiar traits of character.

His amorous disposition and attractive looks made him one of the infamous lovers in history.

The legendary Giacomo Casanova was born in Venice, Italy in 1725 to actress Zanetta Farussi and actor dancer Gaetano Casanova. He was the eldest of the six children. The city of Venice was the pleasure capital of Europe at the time of Casanova's birth. The powerful socio-religious elites tolerated many vices and encouraged tourism. The libertine atmosphere attracted youngsters to gambling houses and beautiful courtesans. This was the milieu of Casanova's life that made him its notorious, rather reprehensible representative.

Casanova was sent to Padua at the age of nine under the care of his grandmother after his father's death. He studied there and obtained his doctorate at the age of sixteen, a rare achievement for a teenager. He entered the seminary of St. Cyprian but was expelled due to his misdemeanour. Thereafter he spent some time with a Roman Catholic Cardinal but was dismissed on charges of corrupting an underage girl. He abandoned his religious career and in 1745 joined the Italian military. He made extensive travels during this period of military service.

As a child Casanova was very intelligent and precocious. He demonstrated a quick wit, an inquisitive mind and a deep desire for knowledge. He studied Moral Philosophy, Chemistry, Mathematics and Medicine. However he had an unhappy childhood because of the parental carelessness. The neglect by his parents was a sad phase of bitter memory for Casanova. He wrote "So they got rid of me". He spent some time in a boarding house the condition of which was appalling. Therefore he was put under the care of a religious instructor named Abbe Gozzi who tutored him in academic subjects and also trained him how to play violin.

Casanova had the first contact with the opposite sex at the age of eleven in the household of Gozzi. Abbe Gozzi's younger sister Bettina fondled him and he had the first sensation of sex. Bettina was pretty, light hearted and an avid reader of romances. The girl pleased him and kindled in his heart the first sparks of a feeling which became his ruling passion in life. Casanova maintained a lifelong relation with Bettina even after her marriage.

As he grew Casanova became more and more addicted to gambling, wine and woman. He was adept in the art of pleasing people especially the fair sex with his impressive personality, wealth and appealing skill of conversation. He showed a peculiar penchant for good food, wine and sophisticated social behaviour to impress people. Casanova's growing curiosity about women led to his first sexual experience with two sisters Nanette and Marton Savorgnan aged 14 and 16 years. Casanova's affairs like this continued with everyone from married women to nuns and virgins.

Casanova is said to have made love with more than 140 women during his life time. The figure is indeed astounding and alarming by any standard of morality and social norms. He performed his meticulous feat with a magnificent rhythm. Casanova got involved in a scandal wherever he went and stayed. He found out some rich patron for his financial support. He would seduce someone leading to a scandal, get involved in some crime and then would leave the town in search of a new victim. He shuttled between Italy, Germany, France, Poland and many other European countries.

The most interesting aspect of his affairs was that he never broke up with a woman whom he had seduced. The separation, if at all it took place, was through mutual consent. Therefore there was no rancour, no heartbreak, no revenge and no domestic liability but only a bit of sadness sometimes.

Among the number of women whom Casanova seduced Henrietta whom he had met in 1749 was a great fascinating love. She called him as the most honourable man whom she had ever met in this world. They parted company after spending a few days in a hotel room in Geneva. However when they met again after many years Casanova failed to recognize her. In 1769 when she was 51 years Henrietta wrote to him "But will you believe me that while I still love you, I am happy that you did not recognize me? It is not that I am ugly, but plumpness has altered my physiognomy".

Henrietta captivated Casanova more than any other woman. She had a deep understanding of Casanova's nature and his volatile social relationships and above all his precarious financial conditions. Casanova himself esteemed her as a woman who combined beauty, intelligence and culture. She was a woman who would make man happy and satisfied twenty four hours.

The amorous adventures of Casanova were never offensive to the women. He always kept cool before inviting a woman to his bed chamber and favoured sex with mutual consent. The guiding principle of his love dalliance was "Be witty, charming and confidential". Never be a predator and never attack a novice. Casanova valued intelligent women. He knew beautiful women without mind would leave her lover with no resource after he had physically enjoyed her charms.

Casanova

Casanova's affair with Donna Lucrezia began in a carriage ride to Rome. Her husband was unaware of the amorous advances of Casanova. The poor cuckolded husband was oblivious of the response of his wife to Casanova's flirting and dubious relation with his wife. Her husband seemed to have ignored the time the two spent together in privacy. Casanova boastfully claims to have sneaked into Lucrezia's bed and made love with her a few times. He also had an affair with Lucrezia's 17 year old sister Angelica weeks before her wedding.

Leonilda was the love child of Casanova and Donna Lucrezia brought up as illegitimate by her family. Casanova had dark intentions on his daughter and sired his own grandson in promiscuous alliance.

His affair with another girl Teresa Lanti, a beautiful girl who was posing as a man ended up in having a son.

Casanova's affairs were innumerable without any control of morality and social sense. He shared bed with women across Europe irrespective of their age and marital status. He was a great trickster who had marvellous capacity to seduce any woman without any resistance from her side.

However, all womanizing acts were not innocently done. There were cases of violent sex, rape, battery and scandalous relations. Casanova had a penchant for virgins whom he used to assure undying devotion before deserting them. Although he claimed that he had to find his women physically and mentally stimulating, he had sex with complete strangers and even street prostitutes. Many a time his amorous conquests had led to street duels and violence for women. He succeeded in his love escapades because of his brilliant power of persuasion and exceptional personal attraction.

Casanova was a man with ingenious ideas about women and attitude towards them far ahead of his time. He believed that while making love there should be equal exchange of pleasure. This attitude impressed his women lovers. His reputation as an adorable lover proliferated among his lovers and prospective lovers. He used his nobility, looks, charming words and fascinating body language to seduce women in the most calculated way. Casanova wrote frankly in his memoirs "I do not conquer. I submit". It was the greatest secret of the finest philanderer of history, the charismatic Casanova.

Casanova had a fascinating affair with an Irish girl named Marie Louise O'Murphy who was exceptionally beautiful. She posed for a nude portrait in 1752 at the age of 15 years. The provocative painting by Francois Boucher was so captivating that King Louis XV wanted to see the real model. She met the king and the enraptured Louis made her his mistress. Casanova claimed in his memoirs that he was the first to identify the potentialities of the girl when he flirted with her. It was because of him that she became the favourite of Louis XV. Marie continued to play the role of the king's mistress for two years and gave birth to the King's illegitimate daughter.

However, very clever and ambitious as she was, Marie unfortunately tried to replace Madame Pompadour who was extremely influential as Louis' dependable companion. Marie's plans recoiled on her. Marie was shown the way out of the palace at the instance of Madam Pompadour and quickly arranged her marriage to another man.

The great womanizer Casanova died in 1798 at the age of 73, a commendable long life span for an incorrigible romancer and sex maniac like him. His last words were "I have lived as a philosopher and die like a Christian". Casanova's mortal remains were buried in the graveyard of St.Barbara's church outside Dux where he was living since 1785 in service of Count Von Waldstein whom he had acquainted at Vienna.

The last years of the infamous gambler and sex adventurist were full of discontentment. He was increasingly bored, unhappy and often displayed bad temper. The young Count was frequently away and there was depletion of food and services at home. He then employed his last years creatively in writing his memoirs which was published years after his death. The huge 12 volume autobiography of more than four thousand pages reflects his melancholy, disappointments and dejection during his old age. The monumental memoirs ensured Casanova an enduring reputation as a womanizer on an epic scale and as a prolific author.

The autobiography of Casanova depicts the incredible story of the most fascinating lover, rather seducer of history. He travelled extensively, gambled regularly, earned abundantly, befriended fastidious women and spent lavishly on sensual pleasures. And considering the number of women he seduced he might have sired dozens of illegitimate children who might have grown like bastards and rascals born from illicit liaisons.

Casanova earned huge fortune during the eventful years of his life, went bankrupt many times, regained wealth and lost again. However he never refrained from trapping new victims of seduction. Romance and sex were his ultimate weakness and at the same time the causes of the anomalies of his life.

His obsessive sexual passion continued unabated despite his frequent financial downfalls and police records. He befriended beautiful Manon Balletti the daughter of Italian actors performing in France. They started their relationship when Casanova was 32 and Manon was 17. Manon wrote extremely enticing love letters to Casanova whom she addressed as "My lover, my husband, and my friend". Initially Casanova was interested in flirting with her glamorous and beautiful mother Mario Balletti. He left Paris for a few years and went to Venice. There he was imprisoned for his involvement in many crimes. However he escaped from the captivity and reappeared in Paris in 1757.

Back in Paris Casanova renewed his familiarity with the Balletti family. But this time it was the daughter, not the mother who attracted him. It was not difficult for an astute womanizer like Casanova to entice the beautiful seventeen year old Manon although she was fifteen years younger to him. Manon broke her engagement with her music teacher Clement and devoted all her love and hope in her relationship with Casanova. However Casanova was bit nervous and insecure after breaking her engagement. He knew flirting was extremely a safe amusement as far as she was engaged to someone else.

The affair with Manon was not as exciting as those affairs Casanova had with other married women. Manon was a novice in love and had fascinating dreams and aspirations about married life. She loved a life of commitment whereas Casanova liked a life of non-commitment. Therefore he preferred relationship with mature women who could understand the meaning and implication of flirting and love making. Gradually within two years of flirting Casanova started showing signs of detachment. Manon's inexperience and youth proved unacceptable to Casanova. He wanted to be an uncompromising libertine in love.

Meanwhile Casanova continued his affairs with innumerable women across Europe during tours. Manon was desperate and was experiencing the pangs of his first love. She felt insecure about her future and suspected the genuineness of Casanova's love for her. Casanova was busy with his routine socializing and enjoying the heat of other women. His relationship with Manon became increasingly inconstant and precarious. Manon wanted to secure their relation but was in vain. Finally the inevitable happened. Their love disintegrated to a point of no return. Manon returned all the love letters to Casanova and with a broken heart married another man and lived a happy married life and died in 1776 at the age of thirty six.

Casanova was known for his extraordinary amorous abilities and his reputation as the ultimate seducer. His innumerable liaisons with women were very impressive in their details. He followed the art of love making with meticulous perfection. The whole process from encountering his victim to the final erotic love making was well planned and cleverly executed. He was never offensive and irritating in the whole exercise. Casanova ensured that the woman is properly instructed before enjoying the pleasures of the body. He was never in a hurry to ensnare his victim so as to cause mental distance. Casanova was especially careful to build mutual attraction and appreciation. He adopted innovative seductive techniques to gain the confidence and trust of the woman to derive maximum enjoyment.

The great womanizer, perhaps greater than the mythical Don Juan or the unscrupulous Lothario, Casanova employed amusing tactics to attract the opposite sex. Casanova narrated an incident during his stay in the city of London. He had no friends there and was very lonely. He put a notice outside the window that he wanted to sublet an inexpensive apartment in his house to a young lady able to speak Italian. The lady must have no male visitor and must give company to Casanova at the dinner table. Soon Casanova got a female tenant companion, a young and beautiful Portuguese noble lady named Mistress Pauline. Casanova soon fell in love with her and courted her until she willingly made love with him. Casanova asserts in his autobiography that both of them were equally delighted in the erotic pleasure and excitements.

Casanova was a super specialist in the art and technique of sexual advances and seduction. His charm and charisma remained irresistible to women for many years. He gave the world already full of seducers typical Casanova style tips to master the art of seduction. The crux of seduction was his dictum "I do not conquer, I submit."

CASANOVAN PRINCIPLES AND TECHNIQUES OF SEDUCTION

[1] **Make the woman feel special**. Do something unique and different. Casanova had a huge apartment to entertain his female companions and perform his soirees of seduction. He escorted his new victim to his elegant apartment arm in arm with full honour. He played an honourable host and made her feel at home till she succumbed to his carnal indulgences. He told his lovers "You are an option, you are my priority."

[2] **Privacy as the primary condition of sexual acts.** Casanova disliked disturbance when he was with his new lover. The apartment staff members were strictly instructed not to distract him during his amorous amusements. He gave the impression to his lover that he was fully focused and was exclusively hers.

[3] **Admire the lover from all angles.** The apartment of Casanova was set in highly romantic ambience. He appreciated his lover from all possible perspectives. He said "I am in love with your smile, your voice, your body, your laugh, and your eyes. But most of all I am in love with you". He complimented the woman not

only for her beauty but also for her intelligence and common sense. Casanova used to say "Compliment intelligent woman for her beauty, and beautiful woman for her intelligence."

[4] **Ask what the woman feels and thinks.** Casanova captivated the women's minds by asking questions which pleased them to answer. The questions were in the form of flatteries and titillating praises. He subdued her mind and heart before touching her body. Once she was mentally ensnared it was easy to perform pleasurable love making.

[5] **Lavish and expensive meals**. Casanova was convinced that the easy way to the heart of a woman was through her stomach. He therefore entertained his voluptuous women with sumptuous dishes. The meals consisted of palatable dishes of oysters, sturgeon, truffles, champagne, fruits etc. which suited to the taste of the lady.

[6] **Must create ambience appealing to the senses of the women**. Casanova used fragrance and flowers in the room to induce a romantic aroma. The whole atmosphere of the apartment stimulated the indulgent senses of the woman. He was meticulously careful about keeping the woman feel sensual and vibrant.

[7] **Be a playful companion.** Never hurry because hurry will cause worry. Casanova was free and playful with women. He found pleasure in passionately watching the women consume their tasty and sexually stimulating dishes and drinks.

Dinner was an exciting prelude to the "after supper" sexual indulgences.

[8] **Surprise gifts and attractive mementoes.** Casanova was adept in reading the minds of women. He gave them beautiful gifts and tokens to celebrate their love. Such largesse on the part of Casanova fascinated the women. This kind of generosity had an implied invitation to share the bed. Casanova's women could never resist his magnificent gestures.

[9] **Be very courteous, kind and caring to women**. Women respond positively to little acts of care and courtesy. Casanova would stimulate any woman with his bewitching techniques. He ensured spontaneous support to a woman who fell on his lap due a storm while travelling in a carriage. On another occasion he pretended to be a waiter in order to gain attention of his female prey.

[10] **Be fashionable, stylish, and at the same time humble and social in dealing with women.** Casanova was a marvellous person who could captivate any woman through his bewitching behavior. He created the impression that he was the most fascinating man with whom any woman would yearn to make love. A woman once complimented him for his fabulous and stylish clothes. He responded humbly and modestly "My clothes are my way of distracting attention from my face and figure." These words of simplicity amused the lady. She was impressed by his apparent frankness and humility.

We can understand the rapidity and intensity of Casanova's seduction techniques and tactics from his own words, "I spent three hours in conversation with a charming girl. And when I left I was deeply in love."

Casanova was a fantastic romantic lover, a philanderer par excellence who indulged in exhaustive sexual expeditions. He gave romantic love an extra dimension of excessive sex which was exclusively Casanovan style. He was notorious for his sexual explorations and salacious way of life. However he dominated the 18th century as the unquestioned votary of romantic love and philandering.

Casanova's monumental autobiography **The History of My Life [Histore De Ma Vie]** described his splendid interactions with people of all levels of the society including the European royalty and clergymen. He frankly wrote about his innumerable sexual expeditions and adventures of life with great gusto and enthusiasm. He displayed no hesitation to reveal his sexual appetites which he relished without any qualm or compunction.

He was involved in countless cases of gambling, seductions, scams and crimes resulting in legal issues and imprisonments. He had been booked for daring jail breakings and dubious escapades. Nevertheless people appreciated Casanova's genius, creativity, charisma, charming personality and passionate spirit. He established his reputation as an incorrigible lover and seducer to the envy of his contemporaries. Even today people marvel at this man's incredible feats of seduction.

Casanova was a man of sensual and sexual adventures. He achieved harmony and elegance even amidst his profuse acts of philandering extravaganzas. The world remembers him as a paragon of romancers and an archetype of seducers and womanizers. There was one and only one Casanova in history. It is well-nigh impossible to think of another one like him although there are traits of Casanova in all human beings.

FOURTEEN

KING HENRY VIII AND HIS WIVES

King Henry VIII was an extraordinary monarch whose vibrant personality and bizarre character fascinate us even today after the lapse of five centuries. He was the Tudor monarch of England who carved unique place in history through his oddities and obsessions. It was Henry VIII who was responsible for the establishment of the Church of England in 1534 A.D. defying the Papal authority on the issue of the annulment of his marriage with his first wife Catherine of Aragon. Henry VIII had an incorrigible obsession to have a son to succeed him to the Tudor throne. In fact the excessive desire to have a male child was one of the causes of his exotic love affairs and chaotic family life.

Henry ruled England for 36 years from 1509 till his death in 1547. He re-asserted the theory of the divine right of kings and expanded royal power by frequently using charges of treason and heresy to suppress dissenting voice. He either executed or banished even his ministers and people close to him whenever they fell out of his favour. Thomas More, Cardinal Wolsey, Richard Rich, Thomas Cranmer were all victims of his disfavour. He dissolved all monasteries and used the resources to enhance his royal revenue.

Henry VIII was a charismatic ruler according to his contemporaries. He ascended to the throne of England at the age of 17 soon after the death of his father Henry VII in 1509. Two days after coronation Henry arrested his father's two trusted but most unpopular ministers, Sir Richard Empson and Edmund Dudley. They were charged with high treason and were executed in 1510.

History remembers Henry as a monarch who indulged in many chaotic love affairs and marriages. His affair with Anne Boleyn was the most exciting and at the same times the most terribly devastating affair. He contracted half a dozen marriages but all ended in utter calamity. His love dalliance with Anne Boleyn unravels the mysterious nature of Henry's emotional life. He was not a romantic lover in the conventional sense but a strange mingling of bizarre love and sexuality.

King Henry VII with his 4 wives and 2 children

Henry-Anne Boleyn affair must be understood in the backdrop of Henry's love life in totality. His life was a fascinating saga of love affairs, marriages, divorces, and spousal murders. He used his regal authority to lead a licentious sexual life and was least concerned about the hapless women who were the ill-fated victims of his erotic excesses and eccentricities. In fact it was his uncontrollable desire for a male heir to his Tudor dynasty which prompted him to enter into a series of marital alliances.

THE SIX WIVES OF HENRY VIII

[1] Catherine of Aragon [1485–1536]

Henry VIII's first wife Catherine of Aragon was the youngest daughter of Ferdinand and Isabella of Spain. As a child she was engages to Henry's elder brother Arthur as a part of a bigger royal plan of Henry VII to maintain good relationship with Spain. She was married to Arthur in 1501 A.D. when she was just 15 years old. But unfortunately six months later Arthur died and young Catherine became a widow. To avoid the return of the huge dowry and to maintain cordial alliance with Spain Catherine was married to 18 year old Henry, five years younger to her, in 1509 A.D. after obtaining proper Papal dispensation.

Catherine of Aragon

A true Catholic and a devoted wife Catherine had a successful married life with Henry. Henry also loved her and viewed her as an ideal wife. However in spite of many pregnancies and several deliveries Catherine could not fulfil Henry's dream of having a male successor to the Tudor dynasty. The only child to survive was their daughter Mary born in1516. Meanwhile Henry had a brief extramarital affair with Elizabeth Bessie Blount, one of Catherine's lady-in-waiting. She gave birth to Henry's illegitimate son Henry Fitzroy. It was during 1520s that Henry developed a fondness for Anne Boleyn, another lady-in-waiting of Catherine.

Now Henry started showing dissatisfaction with his marital life with Catherine. He wanted to annul his marriage with Catherine. However Pope Clement VII refused to give permission. Henry defied the Pope and took supremacy over the Church resulting in the great schism in the Church. Catherine refused to accept Henry as the supreme head of the Church of England and considered herself as the rightful wife and queen attracting popular sympathy. Henry banished her from the court and she lived the rest of her life in total alienation as a divorcee and ultimately died in 1536 A.D. The English people mourned her death with great shock and pain.

[2] Anne Boleyn [1507–1536]

Henry VIII contracted six marriages out of passion, obsession for a male child, and out of political expediency. As a young, ebullient and athletic man he could attract any woman. But behind every love affair and marital alliance his primary aim was to have a male heir. Obviously when a wife was incapable of giving him a son, he discarded her or brutally exterminated her.

Anne Boleyn

Anne Boleyn was the most popular of all the six wives and many consorts of Henry VIII. She was the daughter of Thomas Boleyn, a reputed diplomat in the court of Henry VII, and Elizabeth Howard. After her education in Netherland and France, Anne returned to England in 1522 A.D. to marry her Irish cousin James Butler. However the marriage plan did not materialize. Anne secured a job as the maid-of-honour to Catherine of Aragon, the first wife of Henry VIII. Her new job profile transformed her life and the history of England.

Anne was a brilliant, charming, elegant and passionate lady. She was sweet and cheerful and enjoyed dice and card games, archery and hunting besides flirting and gossiping. She had developed the fine and sophisticated French etiquettes and manners during her stay in France. Anne was a superbly skilled, energetic and stylish woman at the court and soon became the cynosure of many young men in the royal family. She was courted by Henry Percy, Earl of Northumberland and both were secretly betrothed. However their romance broke off when Percy's father refused to support them.

Henry VIII became enamoured of Anne in 1526 A.D. and began his hot pursuits to possess her. As the maid-of-honour of his first wife Henry has ample opportunities to meet her and talk to her in privacy. Henry made many attempts to seduce her. However she resisted and expressed her unwillingness to be his mistress like her sister Mary Boleyn. But within an year Henry proposed to her and she readily accepted since that was the best bargain available to a maid-of-honour.

Henry who was desperate for a legal male heir wanted to get rid of his first wife. He wanted to gain the love of Anne by making her his legal wife. However he could not persuade the Pope to grant him annulment of the marriage. However smart and ambitious Anne insisted on a legal marriage with passionate Henry only after disengaging himself from the first marriage. So Henry broke with the Roman Church and declared himself as the head of the Church of England solely to find out a solution to his strong infatuation with Anne and his expectation for a male progeny. Many years passed in intense love and finally they were formally married in 1533 A.D. three years before the death of Catherine.

Anne Boleyn had now to fulfil the aspirations of Henry to have a male child. Unfortunately the first born was a female child contrary to the expectation of the parents and the predictions of the royal physicians and astrologers

The king and the queen enjoyed a calm and happy life of affection and attachment. However in 1534 A.D. Anne had a miscarriage followed by a miscarriage and a still birth. Even after a few more pregnancies she failed to provide Henry a male child. Now Anne was gradually getting aware of the dangers hidden in her failure to give Henry a son. When pregnancy after pregnancy failed to bring out the desired result Henry decided to get rid of the unsuccessful wife. Henry had already started an affair with Jane Seymour.

Henry accused Anne Boleyn of charges of incest, adultery, and hatching conspiracy against the king. Historians, however consider the charges as false and fabricated. She was found guilty of the charges during the trial and on May 19, 1536 A.D. she was taken to the Tower Green in London where she was beheaded by a French swordsman.

It is said that before her execution Anne looked calm and composed. She addressed the assembled crowd from the scaffold with the heart-rending words,

"I have not come here to preach a sermon;

I have come here to die."

"Everything they have accused me of is false, and the main reason I am to die is Jane Seymour as I was the cause of the ill that befell my mistress."

The marvellous love story of Henry VIII and Anne Boleyn radically transformed the religious and political history of England. Henry, a smart and handsome prince was a fastidious womanizer, a philanderer who was obsessed with the desire to sire a son. But unfortunately all his sexual expeditions and amorous adventures could not produce the desired result. This inevitably led to cruelty to the spouse and ultimate rejection, divorce and even execution. As a young man his personality was captivating and could allure any woman. Moreover he had enough power and wealth at his disposal. He did not tolerate oppositions and those who dared to oppose him had to part with everything including their life. Henry dominated the history of England during his reign of 36 years from 1509 A.D. to 1547 A.D. till his death at the age of 55 years.

Like many other monarchs Henry too was extremely delighted to dally with beautiful women. It was not love and passion to have someone to share emotions and feelings. It was simply a biological urge to produce a male child as a heir to the Tudor dynasty. He contracted marriages in the hope of getting a dream son. However destiny did not favour selfish desire. Thus one after another his marriages proved unpropitious to fulfil his imperial ambitions. He courted many women illegitimately in the hope of producing a male child who could be legalized later on to succeed him. But there also he met with dire defeat.

Henry had hope in the capacity of Anne Boleyn to fulfill his ambition. She was endowed with a powerful and fascinating personality. She was ambitious and inherited the art and craft of sophisticated courtly manners. Henry was tempted by her diligent behaviour. For many years from 1522 A.D. she lured him but nothing short of the status of the queen could ensure physical liaison. The king stalked her persistently for many years ensure her favour. The history and destiny of England took many twists and turns during those eventful years. Boleyn had become a prominent figure in the royal court of England just like the power once enjoyed by Nur Jahan in the Mughal court of Jahangir almost a century later.

The love between Henry and Boleyn was obviously not romantic and Boleyn failed to beget a son. However the marvellous historic alliance gave England one of the most dynamic monarchs ever to rule England and the best of the five monarchs of the Tudor dynasty. She was none other than the charismatic Elizabeth I born in 1533 A.D. and ruled as monarch from 1558 A.D. to 1603 A.D. for about 44 years. She was known by the nicknames such as the Virgin Queen, Good Queen Bess, The Fairy Queen, Gloriana etc.

Queen Elizabeth I was instrumental in providing stability to the kingdom and was successful in developing a sense of national identity and religious tolerance. It was during her magnificent regime that art and literature flourished in England and the great writers like Shakespeare lived during the period known as the Elizabethan period in literature.

<<<<<<<<<<<<>>>>>>>>>>>>

[3] Jane Seymour [1508–1537]

Jane Seymour was the third wife of King Henry VIII and the queen of England from 1536 to 1537. She was a distant cousin of Henry and was also related to his second wife Anne Boleyn and fifth wife Catherine Howard. She was not very educated but was well-versed in the art of household management and needle works which were considered more necessary for women those days. Jane became a Maid-of-honour of Queen Catherine in 1527. She was meek, gentle, chaste and peaceful in her nature and was esteemed as a woman of the utmost charm in appearance as well as in character.

Jane

Henry was so impatient for another marriage that he was betrothed to Jane Seymour two days after the execution of his second wife Anne Boleyn. They were married on 30th May, 1536 and publicly proclaimed Jane Seymour as the queen but the coronation ceremony did not take place because of the plague in London. Jane was compassionate towards Henry's first wife and her daughter Mary, which made Jane popular among the common people and among most of the courtiers. One courtier called her "the gentlest woman I ever knew" and she earned the nickname "Pacific" for her apparently serene and calm disposition.

As queen Jane was strict and formal and refrained from lavishness, gaiety and extravagance of the household in contrast to the luxury and prodigality of Anne Boleyn. She banned all the French fashions which Boleyn had introduced as the queen. Jane, unlike Boleyn, never displayed any inclination for involvement in political matters. Once, Jane asked for Pardons for the participants in the pilgrimage of Grace. Henry rejected the demand and reminded her of the fate of Boleyn when she 'meddled with his affairs'.

Henry's love for Jane was boundless when she gave birth to a male child in 1537. He was crowned king of England at the age of ten as Edward VI, the first monarch to be raised as a protestant. He was the only male child of Henry VIII to survive infancy. But unfortunately Jane developed post partum complications and died after a few weeks. Henry was devastated by the tragic death of Jane. He wore black clothes for three months as a sign of mourning. Jane Seymour gave Henry a son he so desperately aspired to have as the successor to the Tudor legacy. Jane was a silent victim of Henry's dynastic quest.

<<<<<<<<<<<<>>>>>>>>>>

[4] Anne of Cleves [1515–1557]

Henry's marriage to Anne of Cleves after two years of the death of Jane Seymour was a matter of political expediency and dynastic expansion. He was at loggerheads with Rome and faced imperial threats from neighbouring Catholic France. He needed political alliance with protestant Germany in order to create a balance of power. Therefore Henry decided to ensure the support of the Cleves through marriage with Anne of Cleves whose brother William Duke of Cleves wielded considerable political clout in Germany as the leader of Protestants in Germany.

ANNE OF CLEVES.

From the painting by Holbein, in the Louvre.

Henry and Anne of Cleves had no previous acquaintance. He saw her in a portrait made by a painter named Hans Holbein in which she was depicted as a beautiful demure-looking young woman. When he met Anne for the first time he understood the vast difference between the portrait and the reality. She was not appealing and her appearance was unsatisfactory. After his first meeting with Anne of Cleves Henry is reported to have declared "I like her not! I like her not!" However since the arrangements for the marriage had already been done Henry decided not to retrieve in view of Henry's alliance with William. Henry's adviser, who was later executed, supervised the marriage treaty. Henry was angry with Cromwell for misleading him to a mismatch without proper investigation.

It seems Anne was also not much fascinated by the 49 year old Henry who had also may problems related to health. Henry with his courtiers went in disguise according to the chivalric tradition to meet Anne for the first time. Anne was disappointed with the father-like figure of the man who was once very ebullient and glamorous. Henry was also afflicted with obesity and other ailments. In fact Anne was already engaged to a suitable young man named Francis, the Duke of Barr. She was forced to forsake the alliance for the sake of marrying the King of England.

Henry never appreciated his marriage with Anne Cleves because she was not as refined and sophisticated as his previous wives. The marriage was solemnized due to the pressure of circumstance. He did not like the figure of Anne whom he nicknamed as "the ugly Mare of Flanders" because of her sturdy and unattractive figure. He was not satisfied with the illiterate girl who could not reach up to his expectation.

Henry decided to annul the marriage just after six months. He cited that the marriage was not consummated and also that Anne was already engaged to another man at the time of his marriage to her. Henry blamed Anne's unappealing appearance as the reason for non-consummation. Anne's ignorance and Henry's impatience led ultimately to the annulment of the marriage.

Anne Cleves remained a close friend of Henry and an honorary member of the royal family. She maintained good friendly relationship with Henry's eldest daughter Mary. Anne also reverted to Roman Catholicism in line with Queen Mary. Anne's relation with Henry even after the annulment of the marriage was so amicable that Anne was known as "the king's beloved sister". She spent the rest of her life in England. She died in 1557 A.D. outliving Henry and all his other wives.

[5] Catherine Howard [1523–1542]

King Henry VIII was an impossible personality in matters of marriage and family life. Marriage was an alliance of convenience and family was cohabitation without personal affiliations. Henry always thought of another marriage while one marriage was in existence. Marriage had no sacramental value but had only a value only as a means of producing progeny to inherit the imperial throne. So Henry continued his regular marriage spree one after another making him an atrocious and lascivious husband of his times. Marriage, according to this incorrigible despot, was nothing but a pastime activity to indulge in for sexual satisfaction.

Catherine Howard

Soon after the hurried annulment of the marriage with Anne Cleves in 1540 A.D. Henry entered into another marriage alliance with Catherine Howard, one of the ten children of Edmund Howard who was financially very unsound. Henry became attracted to young Catherine who was a maid-of-honour to his fourth wife Anne Cleves. Poverty of the large Howard family prompted Catherine's parents to send her to the care of her step grandmother, the dowager duchess of Norfolk at an early age. She was young, beautiful, pretty and full of life.

After the speedy collapse of his unsuccessful marriage to Anne Cleves, Henry chose Catherine as his fifth wife. As a young wife Catherine had to face many challenges. The vast difference in their age made Catherine feel like a simple girl in front of Henry. She was two years younger than Henry's elder daughter Mary. Ironically she found the role of a step-mother more difficult and extremely distressing.

However certain revelations about Catherine's sexual life before marriage created havoc in her marital life. The unpleasant details of her past were hidden from the king. As a young girl she had to face the amorous advances of her music teacher Henry Manox. She and her friends entertained male admirers who were of doubtful character. Catherine had sexual relationship with a young man called Francis Dereham several times as a teen-ager. Rumours were at galore about the issue of the virginity of Catherine. The rumours soon reached the ears of Henry VIII and he was infuriated by the betrayal. Catherine also had a secret affair with Thomas Culpepper a gentleman of the King's Privy Chamber. The investigation of this illicit affair led to unravelling of Catherine's clandestine relations in the past. At first Henry was reluctant to believe the gossips and rumours.

But soon there were many scandalous revelations about her past life. Catherine was charged with leading base and vicious life like a harlot with many persons. Her former suspected lovers were caught and tortured and ultimately Dereham confessed having sexual relationship with Catherine. Dereham and Culpepper were executed.

Meanwhile Catherine confessed her crimes and apologized to Henry and begged for his forgiveness. In November she wrote a touching letter of confession to Henry and appealed to his benign nature to condone her crimes respecting her youth, her ignorance, her frailness and above all her frank and humble confession of faults. However all her requests and supplications were only cries in the wilderness. On February 13, 1542 Catherine Howard was beheaded at the age of 19 years at the Tower of London.

The legend goes that the ghost of Catherine Howard can be still seen running along the "haunted gallery" of the Hampton Court Palace. It is said that Catherine was arrested at Hampton Court and the wildly terrified teenager broke free of her guards and ran along desperately screaming out to the king for mercy. She never reached the king who was at prayer in the chapel and the guards dragged her away. It is claimed that the anguished ghost of Catherine repeats this heart-wrenching journey screaming through eternity.

<<<<<<<<<<<<>>>>>>>>>>>

[6] Catherine Parr [1512–1548]

A few months after the execution of Catherine Howard, Henry's fifth wife, he married Catherine Parr in July 1543 as his sixth wife and queen consort of England and Ireland. Catherine was the daughter of Sir Thomas Parr, an official in the royal household. She was widowed twice before getting married to Henry VIII. She maintained a tactful relation with the king and his three children by the previous marriages. After Henry's death in 1547 A.D. Catherine Parr married a former suitor named Thomas Seymour. However she died shortly after giving birth to a daughter. She was a learned woman with a deep religious bent of mind. She wrote books including the famous one **A Lamentation or Complaint of a Sinner** in the last year of her life.

Catherine Parr was an intelligent woman and a loving step mother. She was attractive, vivacious and scholarly. Henry VIII mother when she was working at Princess Mary's household in 1542. She was 30 years then and matured enough to look after Henry whose health was deteriorating due to many ailments including serious obesity. In fact he was badly in need of a nurse more than a wife. The queen was a vigorous supporter of English reformation. Catherine's religious opponents plotted against her and tried to persuade the king to prosecute her. Catherine was intelligent enough to sense the danger and immediately pleaded Henry's mercy and forgiveness. Henry was totally disarmed before the remorseful queen and forgave her.

Catherine Parr

Catherine Parr and Henry had a happy married life although for a short period. However it lacked passion and fascination. Age and physical weakness had reduced Henry's energy and enthusiasm. The marriage was consummated although Henry was occasionally impotent and had no issues by the marriage. Catherine wielded considerable power in the royal household and through her diplomatic skill she maintained good relation among the members of the royal household especially with the step children. She helped to groom them to take over the reign of dynastic rule. Catherine Parr sacrificed the happiness and desires of her life to marry the ailing king and displayed her loyalty and commitment to the crown.

The love dalliance and married life of the most powerful Tudor monarch of England Henry VIII was very alarming, anomalous and unpredictable. He had marital alliance with six women besides many illicit relations. There was no one to question his integrity in this regard. He followed his own norms and standards of morality. After his disagreement with Pope Clement VII and defiance of papal authority he was the law unto himself. However he had strict ethical norms for the behaviour of his wives. He expected them to strictly adhere to the rules of morality in social life. This male chauvinistic approach led to dastardly crimes against his wives and discrimination of women.

Henry VIII had contracted multiple marriages but had not displayed any sign of romantic love towards any single woman. No doubt he had been very passionate towards his second wife Anne Boleyn in the beginning but had a tragic end at his instance. He was a crazy and irrational monarch who exploited woman for their sexual attractions. When one marriage remained in force he thought of a new alliance with another woman. Once he identified someone as his prospective wife his next move was to get rid of the previous wife.

All the 36 years of his dynastic rule were filled with series of marriages, extramarital affairs and execution of unwanted wives. The diabolic treatment meted out to two of his wives makes him the cruellest monarch who ruled England. He was a lustful egoistic paranoid for whom wife meant the only medium of procreation. He used women to try his luck to beget a male heir and discarded them when they failed in their mission. Ironically even Providence did not favour his presumptuous attitude. His undue expectations were foiled when his wives failed to give birth to male children. He was doomed to die without a charismatic male successor to the throne. It was a kind of divine retribution for being cruel and unjust to his hapless wives for their incapacity to give him a son due to no fault of theirs.

Although Henry VIII was an infamous Tudor monarch he dominated the history of England for about four decades. He was a charismatic statesman and a successful ruler who changed the very stream of European history. His Tudor dynastic rule and eventful personal life provided substantial material to historians, literary writers, painters, biographers and romantic story tellers. He had been a rich visage in tabloid films and television serials. The life of Henry VIII and his wives provide ample stuff for research, reflection, recreation and re-thinking.

"Pastime with good company,

I love and shall, until I die."

[King Henry VIII]

XXXXXXXXXXXXX

FIFTEEN

SHAH JAHAN – MUMTAZ MAHAL

THE ICONNIC ROYAL LOVE

"God separates the two lovers, least did he thought
It would become the talk of the town."

The love story of the illustrious Mughal emperor Shah Jahan and Mumtaz Mahal is one of the fabulous love stories of the world. When we think of love and passion of the past many epoch-making love affairs evoke and regenerate with various hues and colours in our memory. We are enchanted by the exquisite love of the adorable royal couple. The love story of Shah Jahan and Mumtaz Mahal is perhaps the most marvellous love story which evokes nostalgic memories in the minds of the people all over the world. It has survived gloriously through the spectacular monument at Agra, the Taj Mahal. This magnificent love story got a world-wide appeal and appreciation because of the mesmerizing memorial at Agra.

The passion and fascination of Shah Jahan and Mumtaz Mahal for each other was not a fickle feeling but a stable life-long companionship. It was an everlasting communion of the couple immortalized through the amazing mausoleum.

There are many mausoleums in the world erected by kings and emperors to perpetuate their names. Mausoleums of holy men and Sufi saints are built by their ardent followers for veneration as places of pilgrimage. Taj Mahal, one of the wonders of the world represents a different identity. It stands as a unique expression of adorable love. This wonderful monument of love is not only an architectural wonder but also an expression of aesthetic creativity which surpasses all similar edifices in the world because of its emotional foundation.

The love, romance and passion of Shah Jahan and Mumtaz Mahal must be understood in the backdrop of the monarchical Mughal Empire which flourished for more than 300 years in India. The dynastic rule established by Babur, a descendent of Mongol conqueror Genghis Khan and the Turkish invader Timur, in 1526 A.D. continued to sway the destiny of India till 1857. The last Mughal ruler Bahadur Shah

Zafar was dethroned by the British in the first war of independence. He was exiled to Burma where he breathed his last.

The Mughal dynasty had six powerful dynastic rulers like Babur, Humayun, Akbar, Jahangir, Shah Jahan and Aurangzeb till 1707. Thereafter the power of the rulers dwindled and there were only titular heads who simply indulged in the life of comforts, pleasure and profligacy.

Love, lust, romance and polygamy prevailed upon the personal life of Mughal princes. Even in the midst of polygamous life a few love affairs of the princes fascinate our minds because of their exceptional passion and unconventional nature. The Mughal crown prince Salim alias Jahangir passionately loved a courtesan Anarkali. Their love caused extreme sense of revulsion and opposition in the royal family. The audacity and stupidity of an ordinary courtesan to love a royal prince infuriated Akbar. The passionate love ended ultimately in a tragedy and Anarkali was entombed alive in a wall at the behest of the angry father Akbar. This magnificent love story was immortalized through the famous film Mughal-e-Azam.

Jahangir had another passionate love. He was enchanted by the beauty of Noor Jahan. He killed her husband to possess her. Initially she refused his love but ultimately practical sense prevailed and she consented to marry him. She became Jahangir's chief consort and virtually ruled the roost of Mughal reign for two decades using her feminine finesse and shrewd intelligence.

The love story of Shah Jahan and Mumtaz Mahal, as depicted in history undoubtedly captivates our imagination more profoundly than any other royal love story. Their love became immortal because of the famous white marble monument of love the Taj Mahal at Agra. The world remembers the enchanting love story as the most adorable attachment of two human beings in perpetual love and devotion. The people all over the world, young and old, idealize the great love as a paragon of perfection and excellence. The story reveals more than history. It makes history an extraordinary romantic experience. Perhaps it is the captivating love which makes Shah Jahan more endearing to the people than his stupendous performance as the fifth powerful Mughal Emperor whose reign was esteemed as the golden period of Mughal history.

The ebullient Mughal prince Shahabuddin Mohammed Khurram alias Shah Jahan was the son of Emperor Jahangir and a Rajput princess Jagat Gosain. Prince Khurram was born in 1592 with a silver spoon in his mouth amidst royal luxuries and grew as the most favoured grandson of the great Emperor Akbar. Khurram assumed the name Shah Jahan or the Emperor of the world on his coronation. He inherited the romantic sensibilities of his father and the extraordinary wit and courage of his mother. He was brought up in the congenial royal ambience of the palace and lived a splendid life of comforts and luxuries.

One day in the year 1607 prince Khurram, then a 15 year old royal lad was strolling in the lanes of Meena Bazaar where the royal women and aristocratic ladies used to gather for shopping. Prince Khurram saw a beautiful girl engaged in silk items, glass beads and precious stones. The bewitching beauty of the girl enchanted Khurram. The girl was Arjumand Bano Begum the daughter of a Persian noble Asaf Khan who held a high profile job under the Mughal. He was the brother of his step mother Noor Jahan. The very first glimpse of the ensnaring beauty of the girl ignited an irresistible feeling of love and fascination in the mind of the young prince. He was infatuated by her inexplicable beauty and a deep passion overpowered his senses.

Khurram was a young and energetic prince of 15 years of age and Arjumand Bano Begum was a charming, intelligent and fascinating 14 year old lass. They met frequently and their passion and attraction for each other more and more intense in the course of time. Khurram revealed his desire to marry the girl to his father Jahangir who readily consented to his son's marriage with the girl. Khurram and Arjumand Bano were betrothed in 1607. However, their formal marriage was delayed till 1612 perhaps due to the suggestion from astrologers and sages regarding auspicious time to enter into a royal wedlock.

There was nothing remarkable about the five years of their betrothed life. How they welcomed and enjoyed their love life during those exciting years before marriage is a matter of speculation. Nothing can be ascertained about any remarkable episodes of their romance and love dalliance. Arjumand might have created a dreamy world of her own about her unexpected alliance with the royal prince. However Shah Jahan contracted his first marriage with

Qandhari Begum in 1609 after his engagement with Arjumand.

There were no scandals and rumours in their love. Shah Jahan might have been busy with his first wife and had no time to dally with his romantic love. Love for the royalty was a concession, a case of magnanimity shown by the kings and nobles. However Shah Jahan might have felt great delight in his romantic relation with Arjumand because his infatuation with her was irresistible and was love at first sight. Nobody can forget the first love. Arjumand might have enjoyed the occasional presence of her lover. She might have got a free entry in the palace as the near relative of Nur Jahan and also as the future queen. Shah Jahan also had the liberty to communicate with his would-be consort because of the royal sanction to their love.

After their marriage Arjumand Bano was elevated to the status of Mumtaz Mahal, a nickname given by Shah Jahan meaning 'the exalted one of the palace' or 'the jewel of the palace'. Although Shah Jahan was a polygamous prince he had deep affection and intimacy towards his beloved Mumtaz Mahal. The other marriages were contracted out of political and imperial expediency and were nothing more than practical companionship to fulfil imperial ambitions. His heart always remained with his first love in the strict sense and persisted there till her death and perhaps more intensely thereafter.

The jealous courtiers at the Mughal palace did not like the undue prerogative given to Mumtaz Mahal. Shah Jahan used to take all decisions related to the royal court with the consent and concurrence of the queen. Even financial decisions were initiated after consulting the queen and getting her approval. The emperor never heeded to gossips and jealous whisperings of the courtiers and the people at large.

The emperor fell in love with his wife Mumtaz more and more intensely with each passing day. It is said that he did not and could not leave her alone even for an hour. They were united by an inseparable bond of love and care. She was able to tighten the bond of love through her fascinating beauty and sexual appeal besides her extraordinary talents and skills.

People across the globe extol the extraordinary love and affection of Shah Jahan for his principal consort Mumtaz Mahal. However it remains a mystery whether it was truly reciprocal in the strict romantic sense. They had an active married life of 18 years out of which 14 years were spent on frequent pregnancies and childbirths. Perhaps Shah Jahan might have misconceived the meaning of conjugal love as simply engaging the better half in regular bearing and rearing children. Mumtaz Mahal was his most favoured consort. How absurd it is to subject one's intimate life partner to uninterrupted pregnancies and the harrowing pangs of childbirths! Unfortunately it was the indiscreet sexual indulgence which led to her annual pregnancies which culminated in her untimely death during the fourteenth childbirth. There is no doubt that it was sheer cruelty and atrocity against womanhood to impregnate a woman without making allowance for her physical, mental, and emotional preparedness.

God knows whether Mumtaz Mahal had all her pregnancies after due physical and mental preparedness or they were forced upon her through impulsive sexual exercises. There is no reason to believe that Mumtaz had derived exciting romantic experience of motherhood and the pleasure and ecstasy of childbirth. If Shah Jahan had shared exclusive intimacy with Mumtaz how it happened that he failed to understand the condition of the weak, frail and emaciating body of his beloved due to successive pregnancies and childbirths? Did Shah Jahan believe that real and authentic conjugal love means maximum impregnation and many children?

No doubt the royal couple could not regulate their family way and control the inter pregnancy interval to maintain the health of the lady. Had they been cautious they could have avoided the premature deaths of their children. Mumtaz Mahal was a hapless victim of excessive reproductive activities which eventually caused health issues. She was exploited physically and emotionally in the name of love which slowly led to her premature death. Then the surviving spouse in distress out of guilt built a marvellous mausoleum to perpetuate her memory. It is sheer hypocrisy and absurdity.

Ironically Shah Jahan had all his attention on Mumtaz Mahal. All other wives enjoyed the comforts and pleasures of the palace without bearing the burden of child bearing and child rearing. As a polygamous emperor he had seven or eight wives besides a harem of more than 2000 women. He could have mitigated his carnal hunger and sexual urges in a manner befitting his royal status. His excessive concupiscence is perhaps one of the causes of the untimely death of Mumtaz Mahal.

There is no reason however to suspect the sincerity of the royal couple's love for each other and Mumtaz Mahal's devotion to her family. She was a committed wife ready to comply with the demands of her 'Sartaj' without any pique or scruple. Mumtaz was a lady of fine sensibilities and mature emotions. She nourished excellent creative faculties of head and heart. She gained the trust and confidence of Shah Jahan through the dint of her merit due to which she became Shah Jahan's most dependable companion in life as well as in state affairs. Shah Jahan bestowed on her the highest honour of the land the custody of his imperial seal which validated royal decrees. Thus she wielded considerable power and prestige in the royal hierarchy. However unlike her aunt Noor Jahan the chief consort of her father-in-law Jahangir, Mumtaz Mahal had no clandestine political ambitions and aspirations. She maintained a popular image of kind and compassionate queen ready to listen to the neglected section of the society.

Shah Jahan ascended to the Mughal throne in 1628. He designated Mumtaz Mahal as his chief empress with the title 'Mallika-e-Jahan' or the 'Queen of the world'. He showered luxuries on Mumtaz with the privilege of residing with Shah Jahan. Mumtaz was given a regular monthly allowance far exceeding the other wives. Mumtaz travelled with Shah Jahan and his entourage during his frequent military campaigns despite her regular pregnancies and related issues. She was his constant companion and trusted confidant even during his rebellion against his father in 1622.

It was during the military campaign of Deccan that Mumtaz Mahal gave birth to the historic fourteenth child named Gauhar Ara Begum in Burhanpur. She died due to postpartum haemorrhage leaving behind a large bereaved family and a mentally distressed and devastated Shah Jahan.

The love of Shah Jahan and Mumtaz Mahal, no doubt, was charming and unique in many ways. Shah Jahan gave Mumtaz his complete and undivided care and attention. His love was deep and so separation from his favourite queen was excruciating and unbearable. Mumtaz Mahal died in Burhanpur, a dreamy town of south Madhyapradesh, situated on the bank of holy river Tapti in the year 1631 at the prime age of 38 years. She had the rare and laudable record of bearing 14 children during her 18 years of hectic married life. Unfortunately only seven of them survived to adulthood including the treacherous successor to the Mughal throne Aurangzeb. Mumtaz Mahal embraced death during her fourteenth childbirth that has become an exceptional example of sacrifice for the sake of motherhood.

The legend has it that while on deathbed Mumtaz is said to have confided to Shah Jahan four last wishes to fulfil. Her first request was to build an exquisitely beautiful mausoleum for her. Secondly she appealed to him not to marry another woman after her death. Mumtaz entreated Shah Jahan to look after her children with due care and love. Her next request was that he should visit her tomb on every death anniversary and pay homage to keep her memory alive. Shah Jahan honestly fulfilled the first request and built magnificent mausoleum at

Agra for his beloved. It is not evident whether Shah Jahan had sincerely fulfilled the other deathbed wishes of his beloved. All other wishes were overshadowed by the radiance and popularity of the Taj Mahal.

Mumtaz Mahal's dead body was temporarily buried in a walled garden known as Ahu khana or deer park in village Jainabad situated on the other bank of river Tapti facing the royal palace. Shah Jahan wanted the body of his beloved to be buried in Agra. Therefore the mortal remains were exhumed in December 1631 after six months and transported to Agra in a golden coffin accompanied by a huge procession escorted by his son Shah Shuja. The body of Mumtaz was interred temporarily in a small building on the bank of river Yamuna while the construction of the Taj Mahal was in progress. Finally, on completion of the marvellous mausoleum, her mortal remains were shifted to Taj Mahal in 1648 A.D.

Shah Jahan's glorified love for Mumtaz splendidly reflected in the incredibly beautiful Taj Mahal. The deathbed wish of the queen thus materialized in the form of a magnificent mausoleum. The incomparable love of the royal couple gave the world the most enchanting monument where thousands of tourists from far and wide visit every year and return with nostalgic memories. A visitor to the Taj gets the lasting impressions of the sad old idyllic tales of the royal romantic love. It was the farsightedness and romantic vision of Shah Jahan that inspired him to build a unique monument to perpetuate his love for his beloved who bore his fourteen children in quick succession with great pain and who was his unfailing companion through the arduous journey of his imperial aspirations and military expeditions.

Taj Mahal has been depicted as the symbol of deep emotional attachment of Shah Jahan with his most devoted wife Mumtaz Mahal. Rabindranath Tagore touchingly described the Taj Mahal as "a teardrop on the cheek of Time." It is a thought-provoking comment on the monument of love as a man's perpetual love and adoration for his wife.

The beauty and attraction of the Taj lies in the emotional appeal and mystic allusions underlying the white marble edifice. The UNESCO has appropriately acclaimed it as a world heritage site. It was because of the intrinsic power of love that saved the Taj from total destruction and to withstand the ravages of time. However the greedy marauding plunderers had caused great damage to the building till Lord Curzon made efforts to restore and preserve the prismatic beauty and splendour of India's marvellous heritage.

The shock due to the irreparable loss of his soul-mate left Shah Jahan totally devastated. He was inconsolable and remained in mourning for about two years. He was lonely, distressed and companionless.

The sad condition of Shah Jahan gave his fourth son Aurangzeb an opportunity for easy usurpation. Aurangzeb with his imperial ambitions eliminated his brothers including the heir apparent eldest brother Dara Shikoh and imprisoned his father Shah Jahan. Thus after 30 years of rule as emperor he was made a prisoner, ironically by his own son. He was made captive in the luxurious Red Fort in Agra in 1658. Shah Jahan spent his final eight years of life nostalgically gazing at the Taj Mahal through the window of his prison. The only concession that the ruthless son gave to his father was that Jahanara Begum was allowed to look after Shah Jahan in jail and when he died in 1666 he was buried in Taj Mahal adjacent to Mumtaz Mahal's tomb.

Taj Mahal made the love story of Shah Jahan and Mumtaz Mahal the most expensive and extravagant romantic love story of the world. It is not only an architectural wonder but also an edifice with a profound emotional foundation. The royal exchequer had shelled enormous wealth in order to perpetuate the Mughal couple's romantic sensibilities. Thousands of slave labourers were engaged in the construction for more than 20 years to complete the work. Marbles and precious stones were transported from different parts of India and other Asian countries and Europe spending huge amount of money. In order to collect sufficient resources the people were heavily taxed which led to terrible poverty and destitution. One crazy man's love, passion and conjugal fidelity could be immortalized through the monumental mausoleum. However the common man, the royal subjects paid heavily and sacrificed greatly in order to perpetuate the dream of the imperial lovers.

The untimely death of Mumtaz Mahal visibly shattered the otherwise bold and ebullient Shah Jahan. He was utterly shocked and devastated at the unexpected tragedy. The long period of solitary mourning entirely transformed his appearance and way of thinking. When he emerged from the isolation of two years he had his hair and beard long and grey. He appeared more like a Sufi saint with an ascetic disposition. His eldest daughter Jahanara Begum devoted herself to bring her father to normal life. She looked after him like a friend, philosopher and a dependable guide. She volunteered to stay with Shah Jahan in the red fort jail during the eight years of his imprisonment till his death in 1666. The emotional shock and distress of Shah Jahan and serious illness created a favourable condition for his rebel son Aurangzeb to usurp power. He eliminated his opponents one by one including his elder brother and heir apparent Dara Shikoh in the decisive battle of Samugarh in 1659 A.D.

Our knowledge about the nature and depth of Shah Jahan's love for Mumtaz has been through legends, writings of foreign travellers, court scholars and historians. The nature of love and romance as we conceive today does not conform to the 17th century royal love and romance. There was, of course, something extraordinary and mystic in the love of Shah Jahan and Mumtaz that was far from flamboyant and fickle romance. They nurtured love as the primary element of lifelong commitment and devotion. It may be unjust to denigrate their love as mere flirting and dalliance in fine sentiments. Although their love was love at first sight they did not indulge in trifle philandering acts. They patiently waited for five years before marriage in compliance with the decision of the elders including Jahangir.

The magnificence of the love of Shah Jahan and Mumtaz is that it survived the vagaries of time and the intrigues of the palace to capture power. The Mughal royalty was replete with palace conspiracies, family feuds, rebellions and ruthless murders to fulfil selfish interests. The Mughal emperors with multiple marriages had to face the machinations of their powerful wives in favour of their own progeny. Sometimes inordinate number of intractable children fought among themselves for power and inheritance. Shah Jahan and Mumtaz were victims of power hungry incorrigible children who indulged in wars and foul murders. Shah Jahan and Mumtaz loved each other intimately, but could not instil the same love, humanity and fraternal spirit in the minds of their children.

The first meeting of Shah Jahan with Mumtaz Mahal was quite accidental in the busy and messy Meena Bazaar. Although it was 'falling in love at first sight' they had experienced long lasting love. Unlike many other royal love dalliances they consolidated their initial infatuation and transformed it to a stable and reliable companionship. Normally the illusory superficial love at first sight fades with the passage of time especially after marriage. However in the case of these royal couple love grew more intense and charismatic after marriage. History and legends esteem their love during the short span of their marital life as sober, deeper, and mature based on true companionship and mutual acceptance. Although Shah Jahan had seven or eight wives he had a special fascination for his second wife Mumtaz Mahal. She was endowed with extraordinary qualities. She was beautiful, intelligent, talented, supportive, sagacious, witty, dependable and skilled in the art of administration. No wonder Shah Jahan esteemed her as the jewel in the palace.

The childbirth tragedy of Mumtaz Mahal totally disturbed the happy and contented life of Shah Jahan.

He had to face many problems in the palace besides threats and pressures from external enemies. Mumtaz Mahal had always stood firmly in support of her husband during critical situations. Mumtaz might have felt great pain during the last many hours at the end of her life. She might have surrendered to the inevitable destiny with the ecstasy a half-lived life. The last hours of excruciating pain of the beloved caused deep sense of devastation and dejection in Shah Jahan. When we read their story we are overwhelmed by the feeling of pain and melancholy. This renders the story the effect of a Shakespearean tragedy.

The iconic love of the royal couple Shah Jahan and Mumtaz Mahal remains the 'talk of the world' even after three and a half centuries. The people of successive generations including historians, academicians, leaders, writers and tourists have created a veritable halo of adoration around their love. The love of the rulers and nobles is always fair and fabulous. On the contrary the love of the common folk is ludicrous and forbidden like Eve's apple. A huge legion of poets and writers extolled the royal love and gave it the image of exaggerated glory. The royal love was fictionalized and cultivated in a legendary manner. Love as they loved was inculcated even in the minds of school children through descriptions of the monumental mausoleum Taj Mahal. It is time to inculcate the habit of viewing the so-called love of the imperial rulers in the right perspective.

xxxxxxxxxxxx

POSTSCRIPT

All romantic love legends have a common thread of emotional bonding. It is through this bond that we identify ourselves with the fabulous passions and sentiments of the lovers of the past. The foregoing chapters on the passionate love legends of the past encapsulate some of the popular love stories. They comprise of mythological and historical love legends which had lasting impact on human history. The stories are rendered as they are popularly transmitted from one generation to another through oral and written communications. These stories are not exhaustive and are only a few selected from the enormous stock of thousands of popular love legends.

The content of the book is basically intended to render the historically popular love stories. The very first chapter is on the mythological love legend of Cupid and Psyche because folk tales and mythology are seminal vehicles of love, romance and erotic passions. The characters of mythology are gods, goddesses, demi-gods and superhuman powers. They are akin to love, lust, marriage and procreation of progeny just as humans do. Hence we come across marvellous love stories in the mythologies of various countries and cultures.

When we pass from mythology to concrete history, love stories become more and more lucid and fascinating. We get the real emotional impression of the story. The agonies and sufferings of the lovers overwhelm us and we experience the tragedy of the lovers as our own tragedy under similar circumstances. Thus the popular love legends are capable of captivating our minds. They can inspire, insinuate and inculcate stimulating thoughts in the minds of the readers and listeners of fabulous love stories.

The love stories incorporated in this collection are selection from popular legends known to all. The purpose of this book is to refresh and recollect those stories. They belong to different levels and ranges in their appeal and attraction. Some legends are tragic, and some exhilarating to read; some are requited while some others are unrequited; some stories are erotic while some others are ecstatic; some are normal, others are abnormal. However many love legends, although passionate in spirit and appeal, verge on scandalous provocations.

The love affairs of Helen and Paris, King Roderick and Florinda, Giacomo Casanova, King Henry VIII, and the affairs of scores of lovers like them are immoral sexual scandals. There are painful love stories like the heart-rending legends of Romeo and Juliet, Hero and Leander, Layla and Majnun, Salim and Anarkali, and Abelard and Heloise. They enrapture us because of their inherent power to captivate our sentiments and feelings. There are also exceptional love stories which are abnormal deviations of normal love and romance. The bizarre love story of Mad Joanna and Handsome Philip is a fantastic story of sexual abnormalities and psychic disorders. There are many such exotic love legends in history. They are popular although they are disgusting and distressing. Many love legends like those of William Booth and Catherine Mumford, Dante and Beatrice, take romantic love to ecstatic heights. Their legends transcend the carnal temptations and render a divine tinge to romantic love.

The passionate love legends of the past are immortal sagas of romantic love. They are unique and unparalleled. They are universal because human nature is identical everywhere in many ways. All men and women are romantically inclined and therefore exhibit irresistible thirst for sexual and emotional satisfaction. The love legends are the sources of many great literary creations and in order to follow the literary traditions it is important to learn the legendary love stories of the past. Love legends are the rich and abundant heritage and cultural legacy of a nation.

There can be no end to passionate love stories. Human society will simply be an anomalous conglomeration of men and women without exciting stories of love and romance. Love stories will continue to emerge, exist and flourish profusely so far as there are passionate men and women on this earth.

<<THE END>>